BREAK POINT

JAMES PATTERSON is one of the best-known and biggest-selling writers of all time. His books have sold in excess of 300 million copies worldwide and he has been the most borrowed author in UK libraries for the past nine years in a row. He is the author of some of the most popular series of the past two decades – the Alex Cross, Women's Murder Club, Detective Michael Bennett and Private novels – and he has written many other number one bestsellers including romance novels and stand-alone thrillers.

James is passionate about encouraging children to read. Inspired by his own son who was a reluctant reader, he also writes a range of books for young readers including the Middle School, I Funny, Treasure Hunters, House of Robots, Confessions and Maximum Ride series. James is the proud sponsor of the World Book Day Award and has donated millions in grants to independent bookshops. He lives in Florida with his wife and son.

BOOK**SHOTS**

STORIES AT THE SPEED OF LIFE

What you are holding in your hands right now is no ordinary book, it's a BookShot.

BookShots are page-turning stories by James Patterson and other writers that can be read in one sitting.

Each and every one is fast-paced, 100% story-driven; a shot of pure entertainment guaranteed to satisfy.

Available as new, compact paperbacks, ebooks and audio, everywhere books are sold.

BookShots – the ultimate form of storytelling. From the ultimate storyteller.

BREAK POINT

JAMES PATTERSON

WITH LEE STONE

BOOK**SHOTS**

3 5 7 9 10 8 6 4 2

BookShots
20 Vauxhall Bridge Road
London SW1V 2SA

BookShots is part of the Penguin Random House
group of companies whose addresses can be found at
global.penguinrandomhouse.com

Penguin
Random House
UK

First published by BookShots in 2016

www.penguin.co.uk

A CIP catalogue record for this book is available
from the British Library.

ISBN 9781786530134

Typeset in (Garamond Premier Pro 11/15.5 pt) in
India by Thomson Digital Pvt Ltd, Noida Delhi

Printed and bound in Great Britain by Clays Ltd, St Ives Plc

MIX
Paper from
responsible sources
FSC® C018179

Penguin Random House is committed to a sustainable future
for our business, our readers and our planet. This book is made
from Forest Stewardship Council® certified paper.

BREAK POINT

PROLOGUE

THE MOSQUITO'S WINGS BEAT six hundred times per second as it slowly laboured across the hot clay. Accordingly, a ripple of tiny vibrations pulsed out through the thick afternoon air, buzzing and whining over the silent crowd. They had stopped shuffling. Stopped fanning themselves with newspapers and adjusting their oversized sunglasses. Stopped breathing, almost.

Because this was the moment of truth.

The afternoon sun beat down on Roland Garros Stadium and from the back row the two players were a mirage, blurred and swaying in the summer heat. They looked like old-fashioned gunslingers as they faced each other on the dirt.

The last two standing.

Kirsten Keller was twenty-three years old, and seconds away from becoming French Open Champion.

At the far end of the court, Marta Basilia was on the ropes. The world number one was a gnarly oak from Georgian farming stock. The old guard. They used to say she was unbeatable. These days, not so much. Plenty of pundits said she was heading for the inevitable downward slope that would only end when she became a pundit herself.

Meanwhile, Keller was an all-American superwoman. Young, supple, graceful and impossibly fast. The new breed. Basilia hated everything about her, from the blonde hair to the perfect bronzed skin, and the doe-eyed post-match interviews, and the impossible topspin she could whip through her forehand, and the squeals and grunts she exploded into every damn shot. And now she was winning. More and more. Audacious bitch.

The court clocks showed a gruelling two hours and seven minutes; neon-yellow measuring every minute of pain. Neither woman had given an inch. They were slick with sweat and blowing hard, but their steely eyes stayed cold. A lifetime of commitment weighed heavily on their backs. Their fans expected. So did their families. And their nations. And every losing gambler with a Twitter account and a nasty streak was lurking, just waiting to slay them if they lost.

Don't back down now.

The mosquito reached the far side of the court and came to rest on a fat man in the front row. The high-pitched hum stopped. The fat man forgot where he was and slapped hard at the insect, yelping as his hand connected with his own skin. A mushroom puff of nervous laughter bloomed across the crowd.

The umpire leaned forward in his chair and said, 'S'il vous plaît, messieurs-dames.'

The crowd settled, their eyes drawing back to the court and resting on Kirsten Keller's clinging white vest, slick tanned thighs and the bead of sweat rolling down the bridge of her nose. She bounced the ball twice just inside the chipped and smudged chalk line and blew out, long and hard, until she felt as calm as she could.

One more shot. Then it's all over.

She rocked back on her heels, a movement that began an unstoppable sequence. Muscle memory based on years of repeating the same complex series of movements she had practised since she was three years old.

She bent her knees, her right elbow heading backwards like an archer. Her left hand rose in one fluid movement, fingers stretching upwards as she released the ball towards the sky, simultaneously propelling her body forward so that her momentum would drive through the ball like a piston head. Her wrist twisted at the last millisecond to spin the ball and force it high past Basilia's outstretched racket, to thump hard on the cushioned tarpaulin at the far end of the court.

Except she never got that far, because as the ball left her hand a photographer clicked his camera and the noise of the shutter snapped across the silent court like a machine gun. Keller screamed. Not her usual ecstatic squeal, but a terrified primal noise that rang out around the stadium. She dropped her racket as if it were electrified and flung herself to the ground.

And then nobody did anything. The crowd stayed silent, with no idea how to react. Basilia eyed Keller suspiciously, wondering if this was some weird new mind-game. But it wasn't. After what seemed like for ever, Kirsten Keller got to her feet. She was covered in red dust from the court. Her eyes scanned the crowd wildly, she was gulping for air and she burst into tears. Then she put her head in her hands and ran from the court, disappearing into the locker rooms and never coming back.

CHAPTER 1

THE PINK EARLY-MORNING SKY stretched out impatiently over London, testing the horizon, looking for weak spots. Chris Foster watched it from his office window. He had developed a reputation for being the best in the business, which made him a man in demand. Quiet moments like this were rare, so he let himself enjoy the calm. He watched the city pulling at the edges of the pastel clouds, and waited to see what the new day would bring.

Foster was sitting in a Knightsbridge office building that housed a bunch of high-end services: legal, medical, and his own offering of investigation and protection. It was the same job he used to do for the Metropolitan Police, only the pay was a million times better and so far he hadn't been shot or stabbed, or worse.

He sat behind an uncluttered glass-topped desk wearing an expensive charcoal suit and a fresh white shirt. No tie. Two buttons open at the neck. Same as every other day. Twenty-four hours of stubble, courtesy of a late job watching the back of an Indian steel magnate; but he wore good cologne and his dark-brown hair was cut short and tidy.

His assistant, Danny, walked through his open door with coffee and the morning papers. The three clocks on the wall between them ticked a little too loudly, chasing different time zones around the world.

The phone rang in the outer office and Danny headed back and picked it up by the third ring. The assistant's young face was unreadable and Foster smiled; he'd learned well, for when Danny had started he'd been too emotional and reactive. Now he took everything in his stride.

Without a word to the caller, Danny looked up at Foster. 'Tom Abbot?'

Foster instantly leaned forward. He hadn't heard that name for over three years, but it was a welcome surprise. Tom Abbot had always been a good man, and an even better officer. 'Yeah, Danny. Put him through.'

Foster tucked the receiver under his chin and turned his back on the seductive morning sky. Three years ago the two men had sat next to each other in a Metropolitan Police office with no windows and no sky. He almost felt embarrassed by his view these days.

'Abbot,' Foster said.

'Alright, Sarge?'

'There's definitely no need to call me Sarge,' Foster said. 'That was a long time ago.'

'Fair enough.'

'That's unless I need to pull rank at any point in the future, in which case you'll do as you're told.'

They both laughed, because it was an honest joke.

'How's your arm?' Abbot asked.

'Still attached.'

Under the tailored fit of Foster's suit, vicious scars traced the lines that the surgeons had cut in order to attach titanium plates to his radius and ulna, and his humerus and clavicle; which was lot of words for a lot of pain and the end of his police career. It was the end of something much more, too. It was the end of Elaina.

'I heard you left the Met,' Foster said, letting the unwelcome memories dissipate. 'So how can I help you?'

'I'm at the Paris embassy,' Abbot said. 'There's a girl who's been here for a few days. She's a tennis player.' Abbot paused. Inside the office the clocks ticked and Foster's eyes moved back to the window. Outside the pink-and-orange sky was turning a watery blue. 'Her name's Kirsten Keller.'

Foster, like 90 per cent of the world's population, recognised the name at once. 'The American? What's she doing at the British Embassy?'

'Using the facilities.'

'Using the facilities?' Foster asked. 'You make it sound like she's been taking the world's longest bathroom break.'

Abbot laughed. 'We've got a grass tennis court on the back lawn.'

'Of course you have,' Foster smiled.

'It's the only one in Paris,' Abbot continued. 'She's been training ahead of Wimbledon.'

On the line, Foster could hear the clicking of heels on a marble floor. High ceilings, by the sound of the echo. Abbot was on the move.

'We're hosting her as a favour to the US Ambassador,' Abbot said. 'She had a strange turn at the end of the French Open, and the press have been on her back ever since.'

'Okay,' Foster said.

'That's not the whole story, though.'

Of course it wasn't. Foster knew there were plenty of protection officers in Paris who could keep the press off Keller's back. There was something more, or else Abbot wouldn't be on the phone to him.

'Will you meet her?' Abbot said.

Kirsten Keller was Foster's usual type of client: professional, high-profile, rich. He glanced at his diary. His steel magnate was back on a plane to Mumbai and there was nothing that couldn't be moved. Besides, he was intrigued to know what Abbot was holding back.

'Sure, I'll meet her.'

'Can you come here? She's mid-training.'

'Sure,' Foster said. 'I'd like to see your tennis court.'

Tom Abbot laughed and then the line went dead.

CHAPTER 2

FOSTER TOOK THE EUROSTAR from St Pancras and arrived at the embassy just before midday. It was a grand sandstone building with polished brass signs and wrought-iron balustrades. Inside, a middle-aged woman in a security uniform eyed him suspiciously as he placed his passport, phone and wallet into a plastic box. The woman ran the box through an X-ray machine and handed it back to Foster, just as Tom Abbot arrived down a curved marble staircase.

'You've landed on your feet,' Foster said, looking around at the marble floors and the high ceilings. His gaze came to rest on Tom Abbot. He looked the same, but different. Longer hair, smarter suit, but his smile and slightly hunched frame were unchanged.

'You came. Thank you.'

'I'm intrigued,' Foster replied as they walked further into the building. At a panelled wooden door marked 'Private', Abbot paused and nodded.

'It should be pretty straightforward.'

Foster doubted that.

Inside the room two women sat behind a highly polished antique mahogany table. The curtains were drawn against large windows, and a bottle of water sat untouched between them.

Foster recognised Kirsten Keller straight away. She looked smaller sitting down, but as she rose in greeting he realised that her height was all from her legs. She wore a smart black tracksuit, and without make-up she looked young and vulnerable.

Next to Kirsten was a dark-haired woman who barely met Foster's eyes and didn't shift an inch from her chair. She was dressed in training gear, too, but Foster knew from his research that her playing days were behind her. Her years of training had toughened her body, and she had compensated for this with polished nails and a delicate silver chain, which fell just below the hollow of her neck.

'This is Kirsten and her coach Maria Rosario,' Abbot explained as he quietly shut the door behind them and indicated to a seat. 'Chris was my boss in London,' he told the women. 'He knows what he's doing.'

'Does he?' Rosario asked. 'He hasn't done anything yet.'

Foster turned to get a better view of her. She wore her straight dark hair loose and consequently it fell over fiery dark-brown eyes. Every few seconds she brushed the hair back with her fingers, and Foster wondered why she didn't just tie it back.

'You haven't asked me to do anything yet,' Foster replied. Their eyes locked for a moment, neither of them aggressive and neither friendly. Just two confident people evaluating each other.

Foster wasn't a huge tennis fan, but he knew Maria Rosario had been a decent player until her late twenties. Never a champion, but always a contender. And now she was coaching the hottest talent on the tour. Although at that moment it didn't seem to be making her very happy.

Abbot sat down next to Maria. 'With respect, Maria, Chris has protected Prince Harry and the British Prime Minister in the past. You don't need to worry about his credentials.'

Keller looked at Foster while Abbot was talking.

'He saved King Abdullah from an assassination attempt last year,' Abbot continued, and Foster held up a hand.

'Look, I'm not a salesman. People come to me because they need me. If you don't think you need me, that's fine.'

'I think we need you,' Kirsten Keller said, speaking for the first time. Her voice was soft but held an air of uncompromising authority. It was a trait Foster always noticed in people who had found success early. 'I haven't slept for days.'

Foster studied her face. Her eyes were rimmed in red, and faint blue shadows were smudged below them. In that moment she looked terrified.

He had watched Keller's career highlights via YouTube on the Eurostar train. She was impressive. Her explosive power made her look untouchable on the court. Not like the woman sitting in front of him today. She bent down and reached into an expensive-looking clutch bag, pulling out a folded sheet of white paper.

'This is why I need your help,' she said, her hands shaking as she put it on the table between them.

'Right,' he said. 'Let's see what we've got.'

He was less than careful with the paper, making a point of creasing it slightly as he handled it. All designed to say to Keller, *It's just a piece of paper.*

The page contained a small, neatly typed message: *Good luck in the final. I'm coming.* There was also a loose memory stick along with it. It had been attached to the note and there was a tear where Keller had pulled it off. Next to that, a lock of hair was crudely taped onto the paper.

'What's on the memory stick?' Foster asked.

'A video of my parents' house,' Keller said.

Foster studied the words. Not much to go on.

'It's horrible, isn't it?' Keller said quietly.

Foster looked at her and smiled softly. 'I promise I've seen a lot worst. Do you think they were in the grounds when they recorded the video?'

Keller looked surprised by the question, then thought about it. 'No, I think they were filming from the street. But you can see my mom in the window.'

Foster nodded. 'And the hair?'

'My dog,' she said. 'The police tested it and it's definitely dog hair. There's no way I could bring a dog out on the tour, so Benji lives back home with my parents. Someone took a chunk out of his fur back in the States and then brought it over here with them. We found a patch cut out of his coat, when we checked.'

Foster glanced at Abbot. 'Have you watched the tape?'

Abbot nodded. 'There's nothing there, though, Chris. Half a shadow across a windscreen, but I couldn't even tell you if it was a man or a woman.'

'Okay,' Foster said. 'And there's been nothing else?'

Keller shook her head slowly. Foster guessed her life was pretty routine: a series of arrivals lounges, hotel rooms, training days, match days and then departure lounges, before the whole process started again in a brand-new city. Same meals. Same staff. Same old, same old. If there had been anything unusual, he believed she would remember.

'Did all of this come through the post?'

Keller shook her head.

'It appeared in my kit bag. Like magic.'

'Like magic?'

'During my first-round match at the French Open. I'm pretty sure it wasn't in my bag when I went out to play, but it was there when I got home. That's what scares the shit out of me. Whoever did this must have been able to get access to restricted areas.'

Foster nodded. 'I can't think of many places that are truly private, in this day and age.'

Keller's coach snorted. 'We've been here thirty minutes,' she said suddenly. 'You don't take a single note. You write down nothing. Not very professional, I think.'

Foster kept his eyes on Kirsten. 'I don't need to write things down. I notice things, and remember them. It's my job.'

Rosario snorted again.

'You bit your nail when the rest of us were looking at Kirsten's letter,' Foster said. 'You snapped the acrylic right off, by mistake. You thought nobody noticed and you slipped it into the left pocket of your tracksuit. It's there right now.'

On instinct, Tom Abbot and Kirsten Keller glanced at Rosario's fingers. A flicker of embarrassment played across her eyes for half a second, but then she shrugged and said nothing.

'You also thought I didn't notice you texting a taxi firm under the table three minutes ago, because you think this meeting is almost over. But before you go, let me give you some advice. If you ever meet a close-protection officer who needs to write things down, for God's sake don't hire him.'

Abbot supressed a smile.

'It's a good trick,' Rosario said coldly.

Foster's face was impassive.

'Which bit?'

Rosario shrugged, gathering up her things.

'The eyes under the table.'

'I learned it at sniper school,' Foster said. 'Back in the day.'

'What else did you notice while you were spying on me?'

Foster smiled. 'Surely you don't want me to say in front of everybody else?'

He held Rosario's angry gaze. After a few uncomfortable seconds she swore and then pushed up from the table. Keller stood up, too, and put a restraining hand on her coach's arm.

'This is not helpful,' she said. 'Why don't you wait downstairs?'

Without another word, Rosario walked to the door, opened it and slammed it shut behind her.

'You said you don't do a hard sell,' Keller said. 'And I'm glad. But tell me what you think? Should I be worried?'

'If you're worried, you're worried. That's neither right nor wrong. But is there a credible threat? My gut says no. People who genuinely want to kill you usually get on with it. They don't send notes. If someone wants you dead, they sneak up on you instead of giving you a heads-up.'

'I guess,' Keller said.

'I know,' Foster said. 'But Tom will give you my number. You can call me day or night.'

'So maybe I'll see you soon,' she said.

'Maybe you will.'

CHAPTER 3

TWO DAYS LATER, CHRIS Foster was lying face-down in a small white room, pain etched across his face. His jaw clenched as the woman in the nurse's uniform pulled at his arm, twisting and manipulating his bones and muscles.

'You're supposed to be a tough guy,' she said.

Foster smiled and grunted all at once. It was true that in the force he had gained a reputation for toughness, but this five-foot-nothing woman in her white cotton top and combats had a medical file that told her exactly where to hurt him.

'Seriously, is it too much?'

Her voice was gentle, girlish almost, and her fingers felt soft and cool on his skin.

'It's fine,' he told her. 'It'll be worth it tomorrow.'

He gritted his teeth. Eventually her soft fingers found an area worthy of investigation, and she firmed her fingers up and pushed blistering heat into him, like twisting a knife between his bones.

In the three years she had been treating him, Foster had noticed it was rare for her to ask him about the pain. He presumed it was to preserve his dignity.

They were almost done when Foster's phone rang in his jacket pocket.

'Take it, if you need to,' the nurse said, and she slipped her hand inside his jacket and passed the phone to him.

'Thanks,' Foster said, looking at an unfamiliar international number on the screen.

'Hello?'

Foster heard Kirsten Keller's voice on the other end of the line. He made an apologetic gesture to the physio and said, 'What's up?'

'I've had another letter,' she said. 'It arrived in the post today.'

Foster could hear traffic noises in the background.

'Why are you outside? Are you on your own?'

Keller paused. Paris rumbled on behind her.

'Tom Abbot is with me,' she said eventually, as if she'd made up her mind to trust him. 'I wanted some privacy for us to talk. My coach thinks you're a bad idea. She thinks we should ignore the threats and concentrate on my game.'

'Easy for her to say.'

'Exactly. Another video came, too.'

'On a memory stick?'

'Yes. I'm scared, Chris.'

'The same type?'

'Yes. How am I supposed just to ignore this shit and focus on my game?'

'Do what you want to do,' Foster said. 'You're the boss.'

'Tell that to Coach Rosario,' Keller said bitterly.

'Maybe you should.'

The physio handed Foster a glass of cold water. He gave her a thumbs up and another apologetic look, and she left the room to give him some privacy.

'Tell me about the video,' Foster said when she had gone. 'What's on it?'

Keller's voice twisted, half in fear and half in anger.

'Me,' she said. 'He was behind me, filming me on his phone.'

Foster thought about it.

'Easy to do these days,' he reasoned. 'Most people would just assume he was texting. Or checking his mail.'

The line scratched and muffled and the traffic noise became faint. Foster guessed Keller had the receiver under her chin while she spun around, checking nobody was behind her.

'He had a knife hidden inside his jacket, Chris. He kept panning the camera from me to the knife and back again. Taunting me.'

'Take a breath,' Foster said. 'A big one.'

He heard her do it.

'Can you get Tom Abbot to rip the video off the memory stick and mail it to me?'

She composed herself.

'Sure. It scares the hell out of me to know he was right there and I had no idea.'

Still the traffic rumbled on behind her. Foster checked his watch. Rush hour. A busy Paris street. She was safe enough, for now.

'If you're calling to ask for my help, I can protect you.'

'Yes, I'm calling for your help,' Keller said.

'Well then, you've got it.'

CHAPTER 4

KIRSTEN KELLER AND HER small personal team arrived into Heathrow Airport early on Thursday morning. She knew the ungodly hour wouldn't stop the sharks from circling, but at least she had the satisfaction of knowing they'd had to haul themselves out of bed in the dark.

Keller and Rosario spilled off the Airbus A320 along with every other passenger. 'This is our best chance of avoiding the paparazzi ambush,' Keller said.

'Says who?' Rosario asked.

'Says Chris.'

Rosario said nothing. She was still smouldering in general about the decision to hire a bodyguard, and fuming in particular about the fact that Keller had chosen Foster. They waited for an eternity by the carousel, eventually grabbing their cases and racket bags in frosty silence.

'You know what?' Keller said as she pulled the case onto an aluminium trolley. 'I listen to everything you tell me on the court. Everything. But this is not tennis. It's my life. It's my decision. And I've made it, so you need to get on board.'

They wheeled their small mountain of kit through Customs, Keller pacing a few steps ahead of Rosario and wondering how her coach would react to her firm words. She took a breath before stepping through the doors and out into the real world.

The sharks were waiting, and they closed in around Keller before the security doors slid shut. Rosario pulled up close and both women used their luggage trollies like a makeshift snowplough, bulldozing their way through the intimidating crowd. Shutters snapped and flashlights strobed all around them, and gradually the reporters boxed them in and slowed them down.

Welcome to England.

'Are you looking forward to Wimbledon, Miss Keller?' one of them shouted. 'Do you think we'll see you in the final?'

She ignored the question and kept walking, and from every direction hungry photographers shouted, 'Kirsten, over here.'

She turned her head towards the loudest voice and caught a glimpse of a balding man in his late forties, who seemed to be made entirely of sweat and stubble and malevolence. His eyes glinted as he realised Keller was looking his way.

'What happened in Paris, Kirsten?' The bald guy's cockney accent came ringing through. 'Did you bottle it in Paris?'

The floodgates opened.

'Did you have a bet on Basilia?' another one shouted. 'Did the bookies pay out?'

'Are you pregnant?'

Keller knew that *Tennis Ace Denies Pregnancy Rumour* would probably sell even more copies than *Tennis Ace is Pregnant*, so she kept her mouth shut, her eyes forward and kept bulldozing the reporters slowly out of the way, not running, but walking, and dying inside a little bit with every step. The onslaught of questions continued. The flashbulbs subsided momentarily and she could make out the sweating bald guy again. He looked gleeful, pumped up and breathless.

'Are you on drugs, Miss Keller? Did you get the wrong dose?'

He opened his mouth to ask a follow-up question, but before he got a chance his face screwed up in pain and confusion. His head was thrown forward and he cried out in pain. Someone had thumped him hard on the back of the head and he toppled over on the floor in front of Keller and Rosario. It could have been anyone in the middle of the crush. A dirty trick played on a dirty trickster. Kirsten Keller's heart bled for him. Not.

She knew better than to stop her momentum, so she pushed the trolley hard into the bald guy's shins until his prone body spun out of the way. She didn't feel especially bad about it. In the gap vacated by the bald man, Chris Foster emerged. He wore his smart jacket and an impossibly crisp white shirt. He looked utterly unflustered. His face was inscrutable and Keller could not be sure if he had been responsible for the reporter falling to the floor. Not until his eyes locked with hers, at least. The twinkle in his eye made her smile, which made the camera flashes go crazy all over again. Then suddenly he was beside her and she noticed his frame properly for the first time. He was taller than she was, which was not true of all of the men she had known in her life. He was broad-shouldered; not muscle-bound, but stretching his suit in all the right places. He reached out an arm firmly enough to encourage the Gentlemen of the Press to back off.

Keller breathed for the first time in a minute.

Rosario looked as if she'd have been happier to be torn limb from limb by the paparazzi than be saved by Foster. Which he noticed, and registered, and stored for later. At that moment Maria Rosario was not his biggest concern. He was sharp-focused on every cameraman within twenty yards of Kirsten Keller and wondering if any of them had a knife in their pocket.

CHAPTER 5

CHRIS FOSTER FELT THE warm moulded plastic on his back as he settled into a green chair at the side of Kirsten Keller's practice court. The sky above them was a deep azure-blue and there wasn't a cloud for a hundred miles. The breeze had dropped, and Foster could feel the sun on the back of his neck as he watched Keller going through her routines on the manicured grass. She was wearing her sponsor's burgundy dress, fiery orange and yellow around the skirt so that when she moved it looked like fire was licking at her belly.

She worked on her serve, slamming ball after ball to the far end of the court. The smash of her racket pierced the still summer air with such ferocity that it reminded Foster of his own practice sessions on the firing range. Bullets, again and again – her intensity never dropping and her concentration unwavering. She was the opposite of the frightened woman he had guided through Heathrow. On the court she was in control, commanding and powerful.

As each ball exploded off her racket she let out a gasp or a grunt. She seemed to have no control over it. None of the players called it cheating exactly, but from what Foster had read in the newspapers over the past few days, Keller certainly hadn't made any friends in the locker room over it.

His phone buzzed in his pocket. It was Abbot, checking that Keller had settled in.

'She's fine,' Foster said, scanning the other side of the court. 'She can play tennis, that's for sure.'

Another bullet smashed through the air.

Another grunt.

Foster smiled.

'Did you get the video?' Abbot asked.

'Yep.'

'What do you make of it?'

Foster's eyes swept the court again.

'Anyone who films himself with a hunting knife behind someone's back is the real deal.'

'Think he'll show up?' Abbot asked.

'I'm sure he will. He started with letters and movies. Now it's movies with knives. And he's getting closer.'

'Do you need anything?'

'Not yet.'

'Call me when you do.'

'You know I will.'

Foster hung up and put his phone back in his jacket pocket.

He stretched out and waited for Maria Rosario to say something. He had sensed her on his shoulder for the past thirty seconds, half watching her player, half listening to his call.

'What are you doing here?' she asked, without bothering to say hello.

'I'm watching my client,' he said. 'Shouldn't you be coaching her?'

'I'll coach her when I'm ready,' Rosario said, as Foster twisted in his seat to face her.

'And I'll watch her when I like,' he said, 'which at the moment is every minute of the day. So at least now we both know where we stand.'

'It's my job to make sure she wins this tournament,' Rosario said. 'You're a distraction. She doesn't need men staring at her from the side of the court. She needs focus. She needs to be in a bubble. You're bursting it.'

'She's not going to win anything with a knife in her back,' Foster said, shaking his head and turning back to the court.

The finer points of Rosario and Foster's argument had to be put on hold because suddenly Kirsten Keller was walking over to meet them.

'Everything okay?' she asked in a voice that made it clear she knew perfectly well everything was not okay. 'You two getting along?'

'Like a house on fire,' Foster said.

Rosario glared at him for a moment and then walked onto the court to pack away Keller's kit.

'I'd like to tell you she's a pussycat underneath it all,' Keller said, watching Rosario go.

'But you can't?'

'Nope,' Keller smiled. 'She's hard as nails, vindictive, aggressive and unreasonable. And she never backs down about anything. That's why I hired her.'

Keller threw herself into the seat next to Foster. She was entirely comfortable in her own skin and seemed not to notice the warm flesh of her tanned thighs pressing against Foster's forearm as she sat close to him.

'So, is this how it's going to work? You just turn up and watch me wherever I go?'

Foster shrugged.

'If that's what you want, sure.'

'Of course it's what I want. Don't worry about Rosario. Like you said, I'm the boss. And I want you on board. So do you need anything?'

Foster leaned forward and pulled a black plastic watch from his jacket pocket.

'I need you to wear this.'

Keller took it from him and turned it over in her hands.

'Wow,' she said sarcastically, 'this looks like the height of fashion.'

'It's called a StrayStar. It's got a built-in GPS tracker, and a panic button. If anything happens and I'm not with you, press the button and I'll find you. I won't be far away.'

Keller slipped it on.

'Anything else?'

'Not much,' Foster said. 'Just a couple of ground rules. Wear the watch. Stay around people you know. Don't get caught on your own, if you can help it. And don't trust anyone until we work out what's going on. Can you live with that?'

'Absolutely. If that's what it takes.'

'Have you had any thoughts about who might want to threaten you?' Foster asked. 'Sometimes people have a gut feeling, so if anything or anyone comes to mind, don't keep it to yourself.'

'I've thought about it over and over, but I've no idea who would do this. If anything comes to me, though, you'll be the first person I tell.'

Keller stood up and headed off to the locker room to shower. Foster smiled and shook his head as he watched her walk away. On her own. Breaking one of his rules already.

CHAPTER 6

PEOPLE LIKE KELLER RARELY liked a guy in a suit telling them what to do. Even though that was exactly what she had hired Foster for. He wondered how well the tennis star would take to his rules over the coming days. It was too hot to stay in the sun, so he used the fifteen minutes while Keller took a shower to get familiar with the layout of the place. Just in case. Foster was a *just in case* sort of guy. Wimbledon was roughly the shape of a teardrop, nestled between a couple of tree-lined avenues that curved around Centre Court, a boxy green fortress of a place, with ivy climbing up the sides and the world's most expensive front lawn in the middle. In its shadow was No. 1 Court, a royal green doughnut built of similar proportions. The two stadia were surrounded by a further seventeen Championship courts and twenty-two practice courts, including the one Keller had recently vacated.

Foster walked between all of them, getting a feel for distances and lines of sight. He scoped the kiosks and the souvenir stores, and the pinch-points where thousands of bodies would make it impossible to pass. He looked for shortcuts through buildings and across the courts, so that if they needed to move quickly he'd know where to go. He was almost done when his phone buzzed. An alert from Keller's new alarm. Most likely she was testing it, but Foster wasn't going to take any chances.

He ran directly for the locker rooms, vaulting the security barrier and barrelling down the players' corridor, before slamming through the entrance to the women's locker room.

'Kirsten?'

No answer.

The locker room was a modern facility: clean white walls and a maze of stained-pine benches and lockers. Plenty of corners that he couldn't see. Plenty of places to hide. Apparently Keller had taken a while in the shower, because the room was steamy and humid. She answered on his second call.

'Over here.'

He followed the voice into the labyrinth and found her in an alcove surrounded on three sides by square pine lockers and directly under a set of impossibly bright halogens, which sent tunnels of light through the misty air.

'What happened?'

She looked back over his shoulder and he turned to follow her stare. Between two banks of lockers was a mirror, which stretched from the floor to the ceiling. Written in tall letters in the condensation were the words *ANY TIME I WANT*. The writing was fresh. The bottom edges of the letters were just beginning to run, the way blood trickles from the movie titles on old horror billboards.

Foster moved through the room methodically. He checked every corner and every alcove. He ducked in and out of the showers.

When he was certain they were alone, he came back to her and they sat down in the steam.

'Do you think it's a woman?' Keller asked. 'Considering where we are, I mean.'

Foster looked around the locker room.

'I'm in here,' he said.

She couldn't argue with that.

'Can you tell anything from the writing? You know, like whether they're left-handed or how tall they are?'

'I don't think so,' Foster said. 'Not for sure.'

'Jesus Christ!' she whispered. 'He could have grabbed me. He could have done anything.'

She shuddered and pulled her towel a little closer around her.

'Try not to get scared until there's something to get scared about,' Foster said, his eyes calm as they looked into hers. 'Someone drew in the steam. Nothing more, nothing less.'

She looked sceptical.

'Take a breath. You said it yourself: whoever was in here had the perfect chance to hurt you. And they didn't take it. This is good news.'

He smiled and she smiled back, and he felt guilty because he wasn't sure he believed what he was saying.

'I've got to get out of here,' Keller said suddenly, hunching her shoulders as a shiver crossed her back. She slipped out of her towel without warning and reached forward for her underwear. Foster shifted his gaze to protect her modesty. He turned his back and watched the message in the mirror slowly evaporate. In its place came the reflection of Kirsten Keller, her eyes seeking out his; a little bit coy perhaps, but not embarrassed.

'Thank you,' she said. 'I'm glad you've got my back.'

She stood there for a moment in the mirror, Foster staring at her half-dressed reflection, and then she broke into a girlish smile. In his mind, Foster steamed the mirror back up until Kirsten Keller's soft tan curves were all hidden, and then he imagined leaning forward and writing two words on the glass.

STAY PROFESSIONAL.

Good luck with that, he told himself.

CHAPTER 7

TWENTY MINUTES AFTER THE fog lifted in the locker room, Kirsten Keller was fully dressed and sitting in the passenger seat of Foster's slate-grey Range Rover as they headed north through Battersea and then east along the banks of the River Thames. The car was supercharged, with a five-litre engine and an exhaust that growled and rattled and echoed off everything they passed.

'Where are we going?' Keller asked, glancing over at Foster in the driving seat, his sharp eyes scanning the road ahead.

They were a long way north of the rented house she had been sharing with Rosario in Wimbledon.

'Someone knows a lot about your schedule,' Foster said. 'I think it makes sense to change things up. I'm going to find you a hotel. Do you have a preference?'

Keller scanned the skyline, the city of London framed in the windscreen and growing by the minute.

'Somewhere high up,' she said. 'So we can see people coming from a long way off.'

It was irrational, but Foster understood. He called ahead to the Shangri-La at the top of the Shard and booked a suite overlooking the river.

'I bet you've handled a lot of stalkers in your job,' Keller said after a while. 'Why do they do it?'

He glanced at her, then let his eyes go back to the road.

'Various reasons,' he said. 'But sometimes they just melt away after a while.'

'And sometimes they don't?'

'No. Not always.'

The Shard came into view. It was taller than anything else in London, dominating the skyline, razor-straight metal and glass tapering off into the ether. Kirsten Keller watched the sunlight glinting off it for a minute and then turned back towards Foster.

'I don't think Maria's happy about the new set-up.'

'Not my job to make her happy,' Foster said bluntly. 'I'll try not to lose sleep over it.'

Keller punched him in the thigh as he drove. Hard.

'Don't be mean,' she said. 'She's a good person. She just wants me to focus on my tennis. I haven't got for ever.'

Foster felt the age in his bones and smiled.

'You're twenty-three.'

'Exactly.'

He said nothing. Just drove the car until they arrived five minutes later. He handed the keys of the Range Rover to the valet and they headed inside, through the airport-standard security at the base of the tower. They stepped through the metal detectors and Foster set off the alarms, as always.

'It's more metal than bone,' he said as the security guard waved his electronic wand over his left arm.

'Car crash?' the guard asked as the machine whistled wildly.

'Explosion,' Foster said and instantly regretted it, as he saw recognition dawn on the guy's face. He shook Foster's hand and told him he was a hero. Foster thanked him without elaborating, and avoided Kirsten Keller's inquisitive gaze as they passed through security and took the lift to Reception on the thirty-fourth floor.

'Explosion?'

'Long story.'

They checked in and were told that the room was ready, but they stopped off at the bar because it was too early to be cooped up in a hotel suite. The entire outer wall of the bar was made of glass. Beyond the glass was London. All of it stretched out in front of them: the river and the roads and the train tracks. The churn of humanity going about its afternoon business. Landmarks jutted from the broil: Tower Bridge, the London Eye and the Houses of Parliament. The whole view was mesmerising. Eventually they turned away and settled into plush velvet seats facing a screen showing the build-up to Wimbledon. A young reporter was linking clips of recent matches with gossip and speculation.

Keller said, 'How's your drink?'

They had ordered cocktails. It was a cocktails kind of place. Except that Keller had a tournament to win and Foster had a long drive home, so both of them had chosen alcohol-free options and neither felt entirely satisfied with the result.

'Not too shabby,' Foster said. 'By the way, you're on TV.'

And there she was on the screen, going through her paces on the training court earlier that day. Then inevitably the screen came back to the reporter, who started gesturing to the camera, before he was replaced by shots of Keller at the French Open, throwing herself to the floor and running from the court in tears. Then back to the reporter at Wimbledon, who looked partly concerned and partly amused by Keller's behaviour. Then he was gone again, replaced by the pictures of Keller on the practice court. Across the court Foster could see himself, leaning back in the green chair and watching Keller serve.

Suddenly he leaned forward, because he noticed someone else in the shot. On the walkway between the courts a man in a baseball cap was filming on his phone. That wouldn't be unusual, but the strange thing was that he wasn't filming Keller on the court; he was filming Foster as he sat on his own at the side. In the bar, Foster pulled out his phone and took a photo of the TV screen.

A few seconds later the scene from the practice courts was gone and the programme ended altogether, replaced by coverage of another disastrous one-day test match for England's cricketers. Keller decided to head up to her room.

'I've got a match tomorrow,' she said. 'And I've got a feeling Maria's going to push me hard in the warm-up.'

He went up with her, just to check the place out.

'Not bad,' Foster said as they walked through the solid wooden door. 'Not bad at all.'

The room was luxurious, occupying a corner of the building and framing the city behind floor-to-ceiling windows. There was a grand writing desk and a couple of sofas in the outer room, with a low-slung coffee table between them. The bedroom had built-in cupboards, deep, plush carpet and a stylish ottoman. The marble bathroom featured a walk-in shower next to the glass outer wall, so that residents could suffer vertigo while they washed.

'You going to be alright?' Foster asked.

'I've got a Netflix subscription and a box set of *Better Call Saul* to work through,' she smiled.

'Perfect night in,' Foster said.

He was halfway into the corridor when he turned and said, 'When you close this door, keep it shut.'

'I promise,' she said, and held up her wrist to show that she was still wearing the alarm watch. Then she waved her hand and he smiled, turned and left. He checked the door behind him and headed back to the bar. He ordered a beer and pulled out his phone to look at the photo of the guy in the baseball cap. He soaked him in, looking for clues. The shape of him. The way he stood. The way he held the phone. Because this was the start of it. The hunter was becoming the hunted.

CHAPTER 8

KELLER'S FIRST-ROUND MATCH WAS against a Bulgarian qualifier, and she dismissed her in straight sets. She was supreme, smashing her opponent in less than an hour.

Keller and Rosario met Foster in the players' café twenty minutes later. Keller rolled her eyes as Rosario debriefed her as if Foster were invisible.

'And you need to be on the court,' Rosario said, building to the crescendo of her argument. 'Not driving through the traffic to a hotel room.'

'I played well today. What's the problem?'

Rosario threw her hands in the air.

'You need to make the quarter finals just to pay the hotel bill.'

Foster said, 'That's a pretty good motivation.'

Rosario glared at him as if she didn't have words to describe her anger. She turned her shoulder, to make it apparent that Foster was overstepping his role as security advisor. She took a breath to speak, but Kirsten Keller leaned in and beat her to it.

'I'm staying at the Shard,' she told Rosario firmly. 'And Chris is staying on the team. And you need to remember you're my coach, not my mother.'

Rosario stood up and stormed out without another word. Keller watched her coach go and rolled the stress out of her shoulders.

'Dinner tonight?' Foster asked, as if nothing had happened.

'Good idea,' she said. 'Why the hell not.'

CHAPTER 9

THE IVY IS A quintessentially British restaurant, famed for its celebrity clientele. Foster had booked a table for eight o'clock, and he picked up Keller in good time to take a cab across the city. If he'd been alone he would have taken the Tube, but the Underground was no place for Kirsten Keller, especially as she had changed into a stunning black evening dress.

'Good job it's not a school night,' Foster said, when he saw her designer outfit. It was sophisticated but sexy, cut tight to her waist and daring at the neck. He found it hard not to stare.

'Every night's a school night when you're on the tour,' she said wistfully.

She wore the dress well, and the intoxicating vanilla smell of her perfume filled the cab as they drove. She wore a splash of colour on her lips and smoke around her eyes.

'Walk slowly,' Foster told her as they got out of the taxi. 'And don't stop.'

There was a gathering of photographers outside The Ivy, waiting for the A-listers who usually ate there. They spotted Keller and began snapping their cameras and mobile phones.

'Good game today,' one of them said. 'Can you beat Sam Miller?'

Sam Miller was Keller's next opponent. Foster had to hand it to the paparazzi – they were always well briefed. He held back a pace. He had no business being in Keller's photographs, although a mischievous part of him wondered how Rosario would react to a photograph in tomorrow's papers of both of them out on the town.

Suddenly a young guy pierced the paparazzi like a hawk bursting through a flock of starlings. Foster saw him at once. He was shabby but not destitute, and leery without being entirely out of control. Your standard random nut-job. And he was going straight for Keller. He almost got his hand to Kirsten's bare shoulder, but Foster stepped in between his client and the threat. The young guy had built up some momentum, probably enough to bowl Keller over, but he hit Foster like a fly hitting a windscreen.

Foster could smell the vodka on the guy's breath.

'Fuck off, mate,' he slurred, as Foster's huge fist closed around his shirt collar.

'My thoughts exactly,' Foster said, and he walked the drunk guy away from Kirsten and away from the photographers. He came back to Keller and put a protective arm around her waist, which in all honestly was no hardship, and noticed the smell of her perfume again as he walked her calmly inside the restaurant. Keller looked at him, wide-eyed.

'Everything alright?'

'Everything's fine,' Foster said, pulling his jacket back into shape as they walked.

'That wasn't the guy?'

'No. Just a random drunk.'

A waiter showed them to a discreet table near the ornate bar. Keller ordered avocado with sweet potato and Foster ordered sea bass. He ate while she pushed hers around, hardly making a dent in it. Not good for an athlete.

'What's up?'

Keller looked across the table at him, her smoky eyes warm in the candlelight.

'I guess I just keep thinking about the closeness of it all,' she said. 'You know, someone has managed to leave messages in my bag, and in the locker room. Someone knows where my family lives. I can't help thinking: it's going to be someone I know, isn't it?'

CHAPTER 10

FOSTER AND KELLER SAID nothing as they entered the Shangri-La. The small talk had petered out as their taxi crossed the Thames, and Keller had taken to resting her head on Chris Foster's shoulder as they drove through the dark London streets.

Foster told himself it was part of the job to get her safely into her room, but neither of them really believed that was the reason he was there.

'Do you check under the bed as part of the deal?' she asked as they headed into the confines of the lift. Her delicate perfume swirled around him again, heady and intoxicating. That she had reapplied it in the lobby told Foster everything he needed to know, because after all, who was left to smell it except him?

'I check everything,' he said. 'I don't like taking chances.'

Keller smiled.

'Never?'

She slipped her hand into his as they emerged from the lift and walked beside him to her room. Foster smiled without turning towards her, and when they got to her door he took the spare key-card out of his pocket and swiped it. He took his work seriously and swept through the outer room, the bedroom and the opulent bathroom with complete focus and concentration, before turning back to his client.

Keller had already kicked off her heels and she padded barefoot across the deep carpet towards him. Behind her, the glass wall looked out onto London's bright lights twinkling forty-two floors below. They were orange and yellow, warmer than the ice-white stars in the black sky above.

The smoky make-up around Keller's eyes had faded, or maybe Foster had become accustomed to it. Either way, as she stood in front of him she looked healthy and wholesome and vivacious.

'The trouble with this dress,' she said, as if she had read his mind, 'is that I can get the zipper up all by myself, but I can never get it back down. Would you mind?'

Foster looked at her. He preferred her without the mascara and the lip gloss. She looked naturally beautiful.

'What happens if there isn't a guy around to help you out?'

'That's what Maria's for, of course.'

Foster smiled.

She turned gracefully so that he could get at the back of the dress, lifting her blonde hair and arching her back slightly. He lowered the zip down slowly between her bare shoulder blades and only stopped once he reached the small of her back. The first swirls of underwear looked as perfect as everything else she was wearing: classic black lace bordering satin.

She turned to face him and her eyes were suddenly alive, searching for answers in his. They stayed there for a long moment, halfway between the streetlights and the starlight, both waiting to see what would happen next. Keller smiled and padded off to her bedroom, then returned wearing one of the hotel's robes a minute later. She looked as alluring as any woman Foster had seen in the past three years.

'I'm going to take a shower,' she said. 'Will you stay? I don't want to come out and find a message written on my mirror.'

'You won't,' Foster said. 'I promise.'

She smiled.

'Will you stay anyway?'

'Sure.'

She thanked him and headed off to the bathroom with its marble walls and vertigo-inducing shower. He heard the water start to flow, and soon enough the sound of her splashing around underneath it. He turned and soaked up the view outside. Foster could never get tired of a view like that. He got lost in it, watching it long enough for Elaina to finally walk up beside him and slip her hand into the same hand Kirsten Keller had held earlier. And rest her head on the same shoulder that Kirsten had rested hers on.

'Chris?' Elaina said after a minute.

Her voice. God, he missed it.

'You do know I'm cool with all of this, don't you?'

He didn't know what to say back to her, so they watched the stars for a while, and watched the planes gliding into Heathrow one after another in the clear night sky.

'I miss you,' he said eventually. The words slipped out as he exhaled, no more than a whisper carried on his breath.

In his mind Elaina let go of his hand and turned to face him – the same questions dancing in her eyes that he'd seen in Kirsten Keller's a few moments earlier. She smoothed down the collar of his jacket, the way she used to. And then she kissed him tenderly.

'I miss you, too.'

He could still feel her warmth on his lips as Kirsten Keller returned from the bathroom, pink-skinned and radiant in the white Shangri-La robe. Foster watched as Elaina brushed past her, evaporating into the steam from the shower.

'Do me a favour and stay for a drink,' Keller said, alive and reinvigorated by the water. 'Maria won't let me have one. Watching someone else is about as good as it gets.'

She poured Foster a Scotch over ice, without asking what he'd like, and he drank it. Keller told him she'd have to report him to the police if he made any attempt to drive home. Then she poured him another.

She slipped off his jacket and led him to a chair. Keller handed him the second Scotch and walked around behind him, so that she could rub his shoulders as if they'd been married a hundred years. Foster could not think of a good reason to stop her.

'Are you allowed any vices?' he asked, tasting the Scotch. Both of them smiled as the question hung in the air. She answered by slipping a hand inside his shirt and across his strong chest. Her fingers smoothed over his shoulder until they reached the ridge of scar tissue that ran across the top of his arm.

'I cut myself shaving,' Foster said, before she could ask the question that would ruin the moment. Her hand continued to glide under his shirt and, before they knew it, they were in bed. It turned out that Keller was a quiet lover, clenched and breathless, with no sign of the earthy grunts and ecstatic screams she displayed on the tennis court.

By the time they were spent, the first smudge of diesel-brown light was breaking on the jagged horizon. They watched it kindle and bloom into the new morning. Foster ran the tips of his fingers idly across her skin, exploring her hollows and curves. She purred and sighed, more relaxed than she'd felt for weeks. She re-traced the scar on his arm that she had found earlier.

'When was it?' she whispered. He could feel her breath in his ear.

'Three years ago,' he said. 'Here in London.'

'Were you working?'

'Yes and no,' he sighed. 'A high-profile client invited us over for dinner one evening.'

'Who's "us"?'

Keller was young, and Foster could hear a note of jealousy in her voice.

'Me and my wife,' Foster said.

'Where were you?' she asked, regrouping.

'It was just a quiet night at his palace.'

'Oh, right,' Keller said. 'That kind of high-profile client.'

'Yeah,' Foster said. 'We took a stroll after the meal, just in time for some guy to get a home-made explosive over the gates.'

'Jesus!' Keller sighed. 'What did you do?'

'I did what I would have done if I was on duty,' Foster said. 'I reacted by smothering the client. I took the brunt of the explosion on my arm.'

'That's so brave,' Keller said. 'How was the client?'

'Not a scratch.'

Keller turned on her side and twisted around him like a question mark.

'You should be so proud of what you did,' she told him.

'Well, I'm not.'

Keller scanned Foster's face in the half light, trying to make sense of him.

'Why not?'

Foster took a breath and watched the planes travelling across the sky into Heathrow, but before he could explain, Kirsten Keller's mobile phone began to ring. The phone never rings at 4 a.m. with anything but bad news, and twenty seconds later Keller gasped and dropped the phone.

'Jesus Christ!' she breathed, wide-eyed and gulping for air. 'Maria's dead.'

CHAPTER 11

LONDON WAS STILL WAKING up as Foster drove the Range Rover back towards Wimbledon, with Kirsten silent and ashen-faced in the passenger seat. The low sun glinted off the sides of the glass buildings flanking the Thames, and every second car was a cab. The house that Keller had hired with Rosario was cordoned off and bathed in blue police lights.

'Jesus Christ!' Keller breathed as they drove into the street. A uniformed officer recognised her and waved the Range Rover through. The house was halfway along a poplar-lined street, a spacious old red-brick pile surrounded by a hundred other spacious old red-brick piles. The photographers were gathering on the street outside, and the residents had come out to see what was happening.

'Are you sure you want to do this?' Foster asked as they pulled up outside. Keller shook her head, barely lifting her eyes from the footwell.

'I'm not sure about anything right now.'

'You want to stay in the car?'

'No,' she said hesitantly. 'I want to find out what happened to Maria.'

Foster took a breath and turned off the engine.

'I'm not sure they'll tell us that.'

But Keller was already opening the passenger door, which was a mistake, because she was walking straight into a crowd of people. Foster clicked open his seatbelt and rolled out of the driver's door, so that by the time she'd rounded the car, he was by her side.

'What's happened, Kirsten?' the reporters called. 'Are you going to make a statement?'

A police officer standing guard on the door ushered them both inside, and then closed the door quickly behind them as the cameras started clicking. The entrance lobby was impressive, with thick walls and a corniced ceiling as sharp and flat as a billiard table. The place had been modernised, stripped back to white walls and oak floors.

'How are you, Chris?' a woman with sergeant's stripes on her shoulders asked, as she walked into the hallway. She shook his hand for a moment too long and he knew she was looking for the scars. He didn't blame her. Everyone at the Met knew the story.

'It's the other one,' he said.

The sergeant nodded half an apology and let go, then ushered them through to a bright kitchen at the back of the house.

'How is it?' she asked, pulling up a chair at the oak dining table and inviting Keller and Foster to do the same.

'It's still attached,' Foster said.

'It's really good to see you,' Cullen told him. 'Apart from the circumstances, obviously.'

'It's good to see you too, Ruth.'

Keller looked dazed, and the policewoman softened her voice as she spoke to her.

'I'm Ruth Cullen,' she said. 'I'm a sergeant with the Metropolitan Police.'

Keller just nodded an acknowledgement.

'You weren't home last night?' Cullen asked.

When Keller didn't answer, Foster said, 'Home is a hotel right now. I moved her three days ago.'

Ruth Cullen looked intrigued.

'Because?'

'Because of some threatening letters,' Foster said. 'Stalker stuff. Someone seemed familiar with Kirsten's routine, so we changed it.'

'Fair enough. But I'm trying to get a sense of Rosario's last movements.'

Inside Cullen cringed at her own words. It was crass to refer to the victim by her surname in front of a friend, but the slip didn't register with Keller.

'What happened to her?' Keller asked.

Cullen took a moment to make sure she got her words in order.

'Sometime last night Maria decided to take her own life.'

'How?'

'She attached a cord—' Cullen began.

'She hanged herself?' Keller said, suddenly coming to life. 'No way – she wouldn't. Not in a million years.'

Foster couldn't imagine it, either.

'She hadn't had any bad news from home recently?' Cullen persisted. 'Or had her mood changed?'

Keller shook her head. She would have noticed if her coach was suicidal. She looked to Foster for reassurance and got it, in the look on his face.

'Chris, I'll call you later and fill you in on some of the details,' Cullen told Foster. 'Now's probably not the time.'

Her eyes came to rest on Keller, and Foster wondered what it was that Cullen didn't feel she could say in front of her. Soon they were walking back to the front of the house.

The photographers started shouting as soon as the front door opened. Keller and Foster stepped out into the morning sun to face the growing crowd, but Ruth Cullen put a hand on Foster's arm and held him back.

'We're pretty certain it's suicide,' she said. 'But if the pathologist finds anything different, I'll let you know.'

Foster thanked her and then turned to see that Keller had not waited for him. She was only a few yards away, but the crowd had surged to meet her. They pushed forward around her and she began to stumble back towards Rosario's car, which was still parked in the driveway. She hadn't eaten or slept, and Foster could see that her world was spinning. He had almost reached her when she slumped blindly onto the car bonnet and rolled. Foster dived at full length and got his hands between her head and the pavement, cushioning the blow. The crowd surged forward, as he scooped her up in his arms and bundled them both through the mass of bodies pressing in on them.

She regained consciousness as they reached the car, her eyes confused and searching.

'It's okay,' Foster told her. 'I've got you.'

He lifted her gently into the passenger seat, clicked her seat-belt and then turned towards the press, slowly shepherding them backwards until there was room to close the car door. He turned back to Kirsten and saw that she was holding out her hand, her face bewildered.

'My pocket,' she whispered, horror jarring at the edges of her voice. 'I just found . . . '

In her hand was a memory stick, identical to the one she'd shown him in the British Embassy in Paris.

'Shit!' Foster said, and he closed the door and headed round to the driver's side, scanning the crowd as he went. Nobody running. Nobody wearing a baseball cap.

'Kirsten, who gave it to you?'

It was no use. She couldn't focus on the palm of her hand, let alone the crowd outside. Foster slammed the Range Rover into first, taking her away from the scene.

'Can you remember what happened?' he asked after a while. She couldn't, so he leaned over and took the memory stick from her. He turned it over in his fingers. Someone had used something sharp to scratch two angry words into the soft plastic casing: *You're next.*

CHAPTER 12

IT TOOK AN HOUR to get back across London, the rush-hour traffic bunching up at every junction. Foster stopped once along the way, at a petrol station on the A3 to pick up Haribo and Evian, which he gave to Keller. At the hotel, he settled her on the sofa and made her hot, sweet tea. Keller sat listening to the hum of the kettle rippling through the otherwise silent air and said nothing. He sat next to her and asked her nothing until she was halfway down the cup and a reasonable amount of colour had come back to her cheeks.

'You okay?'

'Better for the tea,' she shrugged. 'Thank you.'

She nestled into the nook of his arm, which he didn't think was a good idea, but he could hardly push her away right at that moment.

'I fell onto the car, right?'

'Yeah.'

'I remember the fresh air hitting me as we walked outside, and I remember the crowd closing in. And somebody caught me as I fell.'

'Me.'

She smiled and all of a sudden she was back in the room.

'Thank you.'

Foster said nothing, but he saw warmth returning to Keller's eyes.

'Well, we know something,' Foster said. 'The guy who's been stalking you was at Maria's place at some point.'

Some of the new-found colour drained from her cheeks.

'Oh my God! He must have been right there in front of me.'

Foster shook his head.

'Maybe. Best not to dwell on it.'

'He was there,' Keller said firmly. 'And Maria's dead. That's a pretty big coincidence, don't you think? I told you Maria wouldn't kill herself.'

'We have to let the police do their job on that,' he said. 'Ruth Cullen's a good police officer. I worked with her for a few years. She never got a case wrong that I knew. So if there's anything to find, she'll find it.'

'Shall we see what's on the memory stick?' Keller asked suddenly.

'You need to sleep,' Foster replied.

'I need to practise. I've got a match tomorrow.'

'All the more reason to sleep. I'll drive you to the courts this afternoon. Do you have to reschedule your court booking?'

Keller felt the words *Maria will do that* forming on her lips, but of course Maria wouldn't.

'Don't worry,' Foster said. 'I'll sort it.'

Once Keller was asleep, and after he had rescheduled her practice time, he called Ruth Cullen.

'It was a pretty grim scene,' Cullen said. 'We found Maria strung up in front of highlights of Kirsten Keller on a loop. I didn't want to tell you in front of Kirsten.'

'Thank you.'

Foster told her about the memory stick and the fact that Keller's stalker must have been at the scene of Rosario's death.

'So what's on it?' Cullen asked him.

'I don't know yet,' Foster said. 'I'm about to watch it.'

Cullen told Foster she'd send an officer to collect the memory stick, and then hung up. Foster pulled open his laptop and inserted the stick. The video was of Keller losing the final in Paris; the soundtrack was of a guy laughing bitterly as she ran off the court in tears. Foster listened carefully. The guy was indoors, somewhere quiet. He didn't sound especially old, but he didn't sound young, either. It wasn't much to go on. The content told Foster what he already knew: the guy was fixated on Keller.

Foster let Kirsten sleep until lunch, before driving her to the courts, where she smashed the ball harder than ever. She spent two hours lost in her game, perfecting every stroke in the glare of the sun and the gaze of the press.

An hour into her workout, Foster headed over to the watching paparazzi. One of them turned as he approached. He was too tall and too thin. He had eager eyes with heavy bags and the smile of a man who had nothing to smile about.

'I saw you at Maria Rosario's house,' the man said as Foster approached, his voice thin and tinny. 'Should I know you?'

'I saw you, too,' Foster said. 'It's my job to keep you away from Kirsten.'

'Not doing it very well,' the guy observed with a wry smile.

'I need every photo you took this morning.'

The eager eyes narrowed.

'I don't think so.'

'Here's the deal,' Foster told him. 'I need the pictures. There are three ways I can get them. You can give me a copy, and we both walk off smiling. Or I could talk to my friends at the Met, who will get a warrant and make your life difficult. Or I can ram that camera down your throat and then kick you around the court, until the memory card comes out of your arse. What do you reckon?'

Once Keller had finished her practice session, Foster drove her back to the Shard and ordered room service. Keller called her family to reassure them that everything was alright, even though she was fairly certain it wasn't.

'Don't fly over,' she told them. 'Every time I see you in the crowd, I'll remember that something's wrong.'

Foster went through the reporter's photographs, scanning the crowd for familiar faces, but none of them proved interesting. The sun sank gradually and Keller asked him if he wanted to stay the night.

'I can't,' Foster told her.

She stood in the bedroom doorway and waited for a reason, but he didn't elaborate.

'You'll be safe enough,' he said.

'It's not about being safe.'

Foster looked at her.

'What is it about?'

'Last night,' Kirsten said. 'I had a good time. Didn't you?'

'Of course I did.'

She padded towards him, just as she had done the night before.

'Do I have to spell it out, Chris? Seriously?'

She came close to him and put a hand on his chest.

'We had a great time last night. And you're a perfect gentleman. And every time something goes wrong, you're there. I could get used to having you around – you know what I mean?'

He cupped her head in his hand, his fingers combing through the back of her blonde hair. He pulled her into his chest and kissed the top of her head gently, mostly so that he wouldn't have to look into her eyes while he let her down.

'The day I got these scars,' he said, 'I lost my wife.'

Keller looked up at him, eyes wide and swimming with a hundred different emotions.

'I saved my client,' Foster said. 'But I should have saved her.'

'Oh God,' Keller said. 'I'm so sorry.'

'Not your fault. But I'm not ready to, you know, move on.'

Keller pulled his hand from her hair and brought it to her mouth. She kissed the top of his fingers delicately.

'I understand,' she said. 'I've lost people, too. I don't want to sound cold, Chris. But at some point you have to let go and make the best of what you've still got. You have to enjoy the life that's left.'

Foster looked at her. She was so young.

'You sound like a therapist,' he said eventually.

She put the hand she had been kissing gently back by his side and stepped into him, wrapping her arms around his middle and resting her head on his chest, so that she could hear his heart thumping away inside him.

'I've met a few of those,' she smiled, as a summer shower began to beat on the glass outside.

CHAPTER 13

KIRSTEN KELLER PLAYED FIRST on No. 1 Court the next day and won easily, somehow parking her grief and powering through in straight sets. Foster sat in the players' box, watching the people who had access to the locker room and wondering if any of them had drawn the message on the mirror. None of them looked out of place, so he spent the second set in the cheap seats, high up in the stand.

He was a perfect grey man, blending in until he was almost invisible. He waited and he watched, letting his eyes settle and trusting that his instinct would kick in if anything unusual happened. But it didn't. Keller won, and the crowd began to shuffle towards the strawberry kiosks, and Foster headed down to the side of the court where Keller was making for the locker rooms.

He reminded himself what a bad idea it had been to sleep with a client, but in all honesty, as he watched her, he couldn't say he regretted it. She was glowing from the exertion of the match, pumped up and beautiful. She kept her game-face on until she was out of sight of the crowds and the cameras, but not much further.

'Was he there?' she asked Foster as they met in the corridors in the belly of No. 1 Court.

'Who?'

Keller stopped and looked Foster in the eye.

'You know who. It's your job to protect me from the freaks, not from the truth.'

'Fair enough. But no, I didn't see anyone in the crowd.'

'He's out there, though, isn't he?' she said. 'He killed Maria and he's somewhere out there.'

'We don't know that anyone killed Maria.'

Keller paused and stared at him. 'There's no way she killed herself. No way.'

By the time they reached the locker room, she was starting to unravel into the scared young woman Foster had first seen in Paris. She hovered by the door. Foster smiled reassuringly and said, 'I'm not coming in with you.'

She smiled back weakly.

'Yeah, I guess that's how rumours start.'

She pushed backwards into the locker room, rolling her shoulder around the door and only breaking eye contact at the very last second.

'Shout if you need me,' Foster called after her. As he turned away from the door, his phone buzzed. It was Ruth Cullen.

'We've just got the pathology reports back,' she said. 'Apparently they found rope burns.'

'You're going to find rope burns, Ruth. She hanged herself.'

There was a long pause at the other end of the line. At the far end of the corridor a man and a young girl were walking hand-in-hand towards Foster.

'Thing is, Chris,' Ruth Cullen said, 'the burns were on her wrists.'

CHAPTER 14

THE PLAYERS' CORRIDOR WOULD not have looked out of place in the city hospital, with white walls and halogen spotlights picking out occasional pictures designed to splash a little colour. The guy with the young girl had almost reached Foster, so he listened without speaking and pushed the phone a little harder against his ear, so that none of the ugliness Cullen was describing could escape into the air around him. There was a stairwell opposite and Foster pushed into it. Once he was sure the girl was out of earshot, he said, 'So you're telling me somebody killed Rosario and set it up to look like a suicide?'

'It looks that way. They went to a fair bit of trouble, too. You ever tried lifting a dead weight?'

Foster chose not to answer.

'I would have shoved a handful of paracetamol down her throat,' Cullen continued. 'Saved my back, you know?'

'So there's no question that she was targeted?' Foster reasoned.

'No question in my book,' Cullen said. 'The department wants to investigate the *panicking burglar* scenario, just to tick it off, but I don't buy that at all.'

'Burglars who panic stab you,' Foster said. 'Or they strangle the life out of you. No burglar ties someone's wrists and goes looking for a beam to hoist them up on, out of panic.'

'What's your theory, Sherlock?' Cullen asked. 'And what's the deal with Keller?'

'She's been getting a lot of threats,' Foster said. 'Nothing precise. No accusations, no demands. Feels like it's escalating, though.'

'Killing her coach would be a hell of an escalation.'

'True, but I'm not sure,' Foster said. 'Maria Rosario was pretty easy to dislike. She was all about tennis – nothing else mattered. No manners, no small talk. She was focused, demanding, aggressive. You get the picture? She could easily have enemies of her own.

'Until now, all the threats have been focused on Keller. Nothing about Rosario.'

There was silence on the line for a minute while Cullen and Foster were thinking.

'I've been imagining a betting syndicate trying to scare Kirsten into the result they want,' Foster said. 'Or maybe a tennis rival or another coach playing with her mind, and the whole thing getting seriously out of hand.'

'Which one's your money on?'

'I don't know, Ruth. But none of them really sound like they'd have a good reason to kill Rosario. Not to me, anyway.'

'Well, me neither,' Cullen said, then sighed. 'You know we'll have to talk to Kirsten at some point? As a witness, obviously.'

'Obviously.'

Foster hung up and headed back to the locker room to break the news to Keller.

CHAPTER 15

THE POLISHED WOODEN DOOR of the locker room opened at the exact moment Foster arrived. Another player was on her way out, fresh from the shower and weighed down by an oversized racket bag.

'Are you the guy with Kirsten Keller?' She had a heavy Eastern European accent that Foster guessed was Polish or Slovakian. 'You'd better go in. She's a real mess.'

Foster's skin prickled and he headed past the player, calling Keller's name. She didn't reply, so he moved further into the lockers, and further into the steam, which was billowing from the showers the same as the last time. He raised his voice, quickened his step, his mind full of images of Kirsten slashed or stabbed, blood flowing across the shower-room floor. But she hadn't made it as far as the shower. She hadn't even made it out of her clothes.

She was crumpled on the floor, but there was no blood. Instead she was surrounded by an explosion of black rose petals, tinged red at their edges and scattered around her collapsed frame. One fist clutched a thick bunch of smashed rose stalks, and her other hand was holding her head. Her hair was covering her face and she was breathing hard.

He sat down next to her in the steam, and for a long while neither of them said anything. Rosario had her faults, but she had been fiercely loyal to Keller and they had travelled the world together for three tough years. They were family. Foster was surprised Kirsten had held it together for so long. So he let her sob, and in the end it was Keller who spoke first, her breathing slowing as she lifted her head to look at Foster.

'Marta Basilia was here.'

Keller ran her fingers through her hair, pulling it from her face and revealing bloodshot eyes.

'What did she want?'

'She brought flowers and said she was sorry about Maria. Maybe she was trying to get into my head. I don't know. The flowers just made me realise that Maria is gone and she's never coming back. This locker room feels so fucking empty without her.'

Foster took a breath.

'I just spoke to Ruth Cullen. They think it was murder.'

Keller stared into the shower steam for a long minute, before eventually turning back to Foster and fixing him with a resolute stare.

'Good,' she said. 'Maria Rosario was a fighter. Now nobody will be able to call her a coward. She would have hated that.'

Foster nodded, and they sat in silence for a minute, listening to the sound of the water falling onto the tiles.

'I'll wait for you while you shower,' he said eventually. 'If you want me to?'

Keller said that was exactly what she wanted, and she stood up and took a deep breath.

'Maria used to coach Basilia before she joined my team. Could she be behind all this?'

Foster looked unsure.

'Switching teams is hardly a motive for murder,' he said.

Keller blushed, because she realised that she should have told him something a long time ago.

'You don't know, do you?'

Foster's face told her that he didn't.

'Maria was much more than Basilia's coach. They were lovers.'

CHAPTER 16

KELLER ASKED FOSTER TO grab a couple of coffees, telling him she needed something to pick up her mood. The truth was that she wanted five minutes alone to process everything in her head, and she stood naked in the shower, hoping the hot water would wash away the dread that had clung to her since the 4 a.m. phone call. But the water did nothing to numb the pain. She turned it from hot to cold, hoping the icy water would blast all thoughts of Maria Rosario from her mind, but it didn't.

Under the pin-sharp jet of cold water, Keller remembered the day she and Maria had decided to work together. Rosario said that working with Marta Basilia was killing their personal relationship and they'd mutually agreed to the working split, but Keller got the feeling Basilia had resented the deal right from the start. Either way, before long the two of them separated in a horribly public break-up. The reporters had loved every minute of that, and Rosario had never been quite the same afterwards. The inevitable destination for all of these thoughts was the image of Basilia standing over Maria Rosario, and Rosario dead at her feet. Keller chastised herself. It was a dreadful accusation and she had no proof. But something rang true enough to make her feel nauseous.

She stumbled from the shower and pulled on a T-shirt and jeans, struggling to breathe. She felt as if she were suffocating, the thoughts and images knocking her off-balance and intuition twisting in the pit of her stomach. She needed air and headed for a battleship-grey fire exit, which she shoved through.

She found herself in a thoroughfare between No. 1 Court and the outer courts and started walking towards the practice courts. Almost immediately the open space did the job. She walked fast, so as not to be recognised. The further out she got, the quieter it became until the walkways were almost deserted and the wide-open sky was all hers. Her breathing became less ragged, and eventually she slowed up until she found a court wall covered in thick ivy. She turned and leaned back, sinking into the leaves like a duvet. After a few seconds she took a breath and looked down. She saw her bare feet, which made her smile.

She was still smiling when she saw the second pair of feet walk up right next to her and stop. Men's feet. A big guy. She realised instantly what a dumb idea it had been to leave without telling Foster. On impulse, she smashed the palm of her right hand against the watch on her left wrist and fired her panic alarm.

CHAPTER 17

FOSTER HAD TAKEN HIS time heading towards the coffee concession, testing a gut feeling that someone was following him. There was no logic to it, just a sensation – born of years of training and service – that somebody was umbilically attached to him, weaving the same path as him through the crowds.

It was the guy with the baseball cap. The one who had filmed him on the practice courts. Foster caught a first glimpse of the man's distorted reflection in the mirrored doors to Centre Court. He slowed his pace, reeling him in like a fish. He steered away from the cafés, where crowds were still milling, and into the shallower waters, past Court 4, then Court 8. He stole glances in windows and doors and watched the guy closing in until he was breathing down his neck. They walked past Court 12, out into the quiet of the outer courts.

Foster turned into the public toilets near the exit onto Somerset Road. He took two paces inside and then turned on his heel and barrelled back out at full speed, straight at the stalker. He struck the guy as he reached the door, taking him completely by surprise. This turned out to be a big problem, because the guy was not carrying nearly as much weight as Foster had expected. Foster hit him too well. Too hard. Too cleanly. The guy's legs ripped out from under him and he cartwheeled through the air like a table footballer spinning on his bar. Foster had expected to use the guy as a cushion as they hit the concrete floor. In the event, he went straight through him, landing hard on the walkway and smashing all of his weight onto his scarred, damaged left arm.

Barbed-wire ribbons of pain ripped across his bicep and seared so painfully through his pectorals that he felt as if they were ripping his heart out of his chest. He screamed and rolled, clutching his left arm with his right. He heard the ring of metal on concrete as the knife fell from the stalker's hand. The guy was dazed, but already struggling to his feet. Foster wanted to throw up. Or pass out. Or both. But he forced himself upwards and towards the attacker, smashing a fist into his throat. The guy twisted away and ran.

It was a slow-motion chase, both men stumbling like drunken brawlers on the concourse. Foster would have reached him if the alarm hadn't gone off, but it did. Years of training fired through his body, and his mind switched instantly to his client. Kirsten Keller. Alone and in danger.

CHAPTER 18

FOSTER MOVED AS QUICKLY as his body would allow. Every step sent new explosions of pain through his arm. His GPS told him that Keller was at the other end of the park, beyond No. 1 Court, somewhere in amongst the practice courts. He saw her a minute later leaning against the ivy-clad wall, a big guy standing over her. Both of them smiling. Foster instantly slowed and relaxed. It was Tom Abbot.

Keller's smile faded as Foster came closer into view and she could see the pain in his eyes. His breathing was laboured. The adrenalin had begun to seep from him and exhaustion was kicking in.

'Jesus Christ!' Keller said. 'Are you alright?'

Tom Abbot could see the delicate way Foster was holding his arm.

'What do you need, Chris?'

Foster held onto Abbot's shoulder for support and Keller stayed close as they made their way back across the concourse.

'I got your call,' Abbot said as he took the strain.

'So I see,' Foster said. 'I appreciate it. Have you got your phone on you?'

Abbot nodded.

'Call the police,' Foster said. 'Ask for Cullen.'

He was in a world of hurt as they walked across the concourse. He relayed the details of what had happened through Abbot, as Cullen listened at the other end of the line. He told her about the guy in the cap, and the knife, and the way the sly bastard liked to sneak up on people from behind. Foster knew he should have ended it there and then, outside Court 12. But he hadn't. One miscalculation, and the guy had gone free. And there was no way to fix it, except to get it right next time.

'Do you need codeine?' Abbot asked when he came off the phone. 'Or something stronger?'

Foster shook his head.

'Shouldn't mix codeine with alcohol,' he told Abbot. 'And God knows, I need a drink.'

CHAPTER 19

FOSTER SLEPT FOR FIVE straight hours that night, outside Kirsten Keller's room at the Shangri-La, waking with the light pouring through the unshaded glass. The unbroken half of his body pulled the rest of him from the sofa, and fierce pain instantly spread across his ribs. He spent the day with a brooding sense that trouble was coming, but it never did. In the evening, he sat with Keller and watched the sun setting behind St Paul's Cathedral, and the last of the river traffic crossing the muddy Thames, and the London Eye slowly turning like the mechanism of a giant clock. Days passed with the same aching sense of dread, but Keller's matches came and went, and she won them all, and nobody came out of the shadows.

Foster woke to grey skies on Thursday morning, knowing that Keller was facing Marta Basilia in the semi-finals, and sensing that if her attacker was going to strike, he would have to do it soon. Foster's body still ached, so he found a tumbler and filled it with water, then gulped down four large codeine tablets. He woke Keller an hour later when the sky had turned to a warm summer blue. She showered and dressed and they ate breakfast in the Shangri-La, before heading across London listening to the Rolling Stones, Jagger's mournful voice setting a tone for the journey.

'What happens if I see him?' Keller asked. 'You know, staring out from the crowd?'

'Let me know,' Foster said simply. 'And I'll come and get you.'

She stared at him.

'On the court? Seriously?'

'Yes, seriously,' Foster said.

Keller looked at him for a moment, studying his face as he watched the road ahead. He sensed her stare and glanced across at her.

'What?'

'Nothing.'

She sat back in her seat and smiled, and Foster drove on until they reached Wimbledon. Keller settled into her pre-match routine and Foster melted into the background, watching everything and trusting no one. He saw the crowds swell on Centre Court, slowly blooming and spreading over the green plastic seats like spores on a Petri dish. His skilled eyes swept through the mass of people, watching for anything unusual. In the end he saw nothing but thousands of excited fans gorging on strawberries and protecting themselves from the midday sun. By the time Keller reached the court, the atmosphere was electric.

Keller lost the first set 6–0, unable to find a rhythm. Her eyes flicked constantly from Basilia to the grandstand and back again, her mind distracted by the baying crowd and its lurking danger. Foster could almost hear her nerves jangling as she sat dejectedly in an olive-green chair with her head under her towel.

'How's it looking outside?' Foster asked, as Tom Abbot appeared by his side.

'Nothing doing. It's all quiet.'

'Okay.'

'Think she can get back into it?' Abbot said.

'She will,' Foster said. 'She's a fighter.'

The second set was ferocious. Keller was lithe and fast, Basilia strong and resolute. Basilia dropped an early service game, but broke back in the ninth. They'd been playing for just over an hour when Basilia held serve to send them into a tiebreak.

Foster washed his eyes across the vast crowd, who were all leaning forward in anticipation. Keller came out onto the court with new determination and fired five explosive shots across the net. Basilia had no answer for any of them, and the crowd cheered as Keller clawed her way back into the match. Under pressure, Basilia went for the line and missed, giving Keller a set point. The American spun her racket in her hand, staring across the court as Basilia bounced the ball, tossed it high and double-faulted. Keller held her arms to the sky and roared like a Roman gladiator slaying an opponent.

The rest was easy. Keller dismantled the world champion blow by brutish blow. At the far end of the court, Marta Basilia looked like thunder. If Keller's theory that Basilia had given her the black roses to get inside her head was correct, then the plan had backfired spectacularly. No matter how hard Basilia hit the ball, Keller hit harder. No matter how precise her angles were, Keller threw herself at the ball and found an even better return.

Eventually, Keller served for the match. Her first serve was an ace, straight down the middle of the court, kicking high past Basilia and thumping against the green tarpaulin behind her. The second serve was almost as good, flying wide of Basilia's forehand. Another ace. Basilia screamed and cursed into the afternoon air. The crowd gasped and then giggled until the umpire settled them. Thirty–love. Halfway there. Keller fired the next serve straight into the net. She stepped back and shook the nerves out of her shoulders. Foster watched the crowd. Nobody was moving. Nobody was breathing. Nobody was doing anything but watching Keller, two points away from a place in the final. She bounced the ball and instead of opting for a softer serve, she put everything into it. Basilia had stepped into the court, not expecting such a fierce delivery. The ball kicked right in front of her, flying hard into her body. She was a supreme athlete, but even she could not twist herself into a shape that would allow her to play the ball. It smashed into her ribs, making a hollow thump that the whole crowd heard. Keller held up a hand of apology and returned to the baseline.

'Forty–love,' the umpire said.

Match point.

Foster didn't breathe. If Keller's stalker had a sense of drama, which apparently he did, then this was a critical moment. A dangerous moment. To the crowd, Keller was looking invincible. To Foster, she was exposed and vulnerable. His eyes scanned the crowd and he was drawn to a movement. A baseball cap, on the far side of the crowd. Climbing the stairs towards the exit. But as quickly as Foster spotted him, he was gone. Maybe it was nothing. Maybe it was something. He wasn't sure, and without being sure he couldn't leave Keller unwatched. *Where was Tom Abbot?*

Kirsten Keller went through the usual routine of bouncing the ball twice, looking once down the court and tossing the ball high into the air. It was an exact replay of the final point at Roland Garros, where she had collapsed and forfeited the game.

Not this time.

She smashed the ball hard down the court. Basilia desperately got a racket to it. It looped high into the air and hung there for what seemed like an eternity. The world slowed down and the only thing that moved was Keller, powering into the court and leaping at the ball like a striking panther. She put everything into that shot: the bitterness and humiliation of the loss in Paris, the anger at the black roses, the grief of losing Maria Rosario. The crowd burst into wild, ecstatic cheers and drowned out the umpire as he said, 'Game, set and match, Miss Keller.'

She pumped her fists, shook hands with Marta Basilia and turned to each corner of the stadium, acknowledging the crowd with her racket held aloft. She looked to the stand and tried to pick out Foster, but he was already moving, trying to get to her.

Basilia headed straight for the players' locker room. Keller hung back, enjoying the moment. She'd undone the hoodoo of Roland Garros. Maria Rosario would have been proud.

Keller wiped her face with her wristband as she approached the fans hanging over the green hoardings, waiting for a chance for an autograph. A forest of hands reached out as she came near. They held out oversized tennis balls and programmes to sign. She grabbed at what they gave quickly and mechanically, wanting to please as many people as she could before her muscles started to tighten. A hand thrust through the crowd, close to hers. More insistent than the others. As she reached out instinctively, she felt something drop into her outstretched palm. Her blood froze as she looked down. It was a delicate silver chain. The last time she had seen it was around Maria Rosario's neck. She looked up in horror, trying to identify Rosario's killer in the tangle of human flesh. But the hand slipped back into the crowd like a recoiling serpent and vanished from sight.

Seeking out the face in the crowd, for a second she caught the briefest glance of two eyes glinting malevolently at her. They were angry and bitter; dark pools of hate and unbridled rage. She turned, panicking, searching for Foster as more fans crowded in for autographs. Her stomach twisted, not from the fear, but from the sudden and complete understanding that someone had killed Maria and that somehow it was all because of her. A guilt she couldn't rationalise flooded through her and synapses fired in her brain, trying to comprehend what she might have done to cause this man to hate her. Who could hate her enough to kill her friend?

She searched the faces of the crowd again, but the malevolent eyes were gone, and although she saw the back of a man break from the pressing crowd and slip through a nearby exit, it could have been anyone.

CHAPTER 20

FOSTER GUIDED KIRSTEN KELLER quickly up the glass-and-steel stairs that led to Wimbledon's Press Room.

'You can shower back at the hotel,' he told her. 'Until then, we stay together.'

They were walking shoulder-to-shoulder, Keller vibrant and alert after winning her match, Foster vigilant and attentive, as Abbot followed two steps behind.

'He's getting closer,' Keller said. 'So why hasn't he attacked me?'

'He's biding his time and getting a kick out of scaring you,' Foster said. 'The question is: how long will he wait?'

At the top of the stairs they reached a security door. Foster knocked firmly and a few seconds later a nervous-looking runner appeared. He wore jeans and a white T-shirt, with a headset hanging around his neck. He had the air of a man who was drowning. He stared at Foster's looming frame with a mixture of annoyance and alarm and was about to speak, when he saw Kirsten Keller next to him.

'Oh, Christ!' he said. 'Did we book you? I don't think we're expecting you . . .'

His voice tailed off as he started thumbing through reams of running orders on his clipboard.

'She's not scheduled,' Foster said, 'but I'm guessing you'd like to interview her?'

'God, yes.'

'I need to see your recordings of today's match,' Foster said. 'Specifically the moments immediately after the match, when Kirsten was signing autographs. You give me that, and Kirsten will give you three minutes on air. Can you do it?'

The runner stuck his headphones over his ears and spoke into the microphone. He glanced at Keller a couple of times, and after a moment he looked back at Foster and said, 'Five minutes – and you've got a deal.'

'Three minutes,' Foster said. 'And every second you negotiate is a second less on air.'

The young runner's eyes widened slightly and he relayed the message to his producer, as he beckoned them through the doors. The wall immediately in front of them was completely covered in flat screens showing different courts and different players, with the same verdant turf wallpapering every shot. The screens were angled inwards at the top and the bottom, giving the impression that they were inside a giant goldfish bowl. Three women were working in swivel chairs in front of a huge illuminated mixing desk. They wore the same headsets as the runner and seemed so engrossed in their pictures that they didn't notice the invasion. The runner tapped one of them on the shoulder and she turned round and slipped one earphone off.

'Hey, Bethan,' he said, smiling nervously. 'These guys need your help.'

She was a thin woman with tight lips that looked as if they'd forgotten how to smile. She looked at the runner like she might rip his skin from his body.

'Half of Africa needs my help, according to Save the Children, but I'm a bit fucking busy at the moment.' Her cold eyes moved from the runner to the group of strangers in her gallery and she said, 'No offence.'

'None taken,' Foster said. 'Come on, Kirsten, we'll head back to the hotel.'

Even in the strange light, Foster could see colour draining from Bethan's face as Keller stepped out from the shadows. Good, let her squirm. His codeine hit was wearing off and the left side of his body was beginning to throb again and he was starting to feel irritable.

'For fuck's sake,' Bethan muttered, mostly to herself. 'What do you need?'

'Whatever pictures you've got, from the end of the match,' Foster said. 'Every camera. Every angle. I'm looking for someone in the crowd.'

'And you want this when?' Bethan said in a disbelieving tone. 'Now?'

Foster explained the deal, the same way he'd explained it to the runner, and Bethan rolled her eyes and started punching time-codes into her computer. The runner breathed a sigh of relief and led Keller out into the studio, with Tom Abbot following close behind.

Soon the screens in front of Foster were alive again, and Bethan was scrolling through images until they found what he was looking for. There were two cameras that had caught the scene. The first was useless, showing nothing but a brief glimpse of the guy's baseball cap in the middle of the scrum. The other angle was better, filmed from the far side of the court, over Keller's shoulder. It was a wide shot, with Keller small in the middle of the screen. The excited faces of the people in the crowd were smaller still.

'Can you zoom in?' Foster asked.

Bethan pressed buttons and the frame tightened around Keller. But the closer they got, the grainier the quality of the shot became.

'Can you loop that bit?' Foster said, as he saw the arm emerge from the crowd. 'And slow it right down?'

Bethan did, and the shot played through on the screens in front of them. The grainy arm punched through, and Keller's hand came forward. And then it repeated, again and again, the arm staying grainy and the guy's face staying blurred.

Foster leaned forward until he was cheek-to-cheek with Bethan, his lips next to her microphone.

'Time's up,' he said.

'Did you find anything?' Abbot asked as they all headed back down the glass-and-steel steps. Foster was quiet and brooding.

'Nothing,' he said distantly. 'Just an arm disappearing into the crowd. Dead end.'

'CCTV?' Abbot asked.

'Cullen's going to get hold of it, but I don't expect they'll find anything. There are too many people moving around the grounds, and we haven't had a good enough visual on this guy to pick him out in such a massive crowd.'

They walked in silence back to the Range Rover, Foster's strong hand gentle but persistent in the small of Keller's back. When they reached the car, there was a note waiting for them on the windscreen. It was typed on cheap white paper, folded once and tucked under the wiper blade. Foster skimmed it and then handed it to Keller while he started up the car. *Soon it will all be over. You deserve what's coming. And if you don't know why, then you deserve it even more.*

CHAPTER 21

THE HEAVENS OPENED AS Foster drove back towards the hotel. Plump raindrops smashed onto the Range Rover's roof like meteors, and red brake lights kaleidoscoped across the rain-drenched windscreen.

'Is this normal?' Keller asked irritably as they sat idling in the traffic.

'Pretty much,' Foster said. The black sky mirrored his mood. The strength was slowly coming back to his arm, but with it came a throbbing pain and an unwelcome sense of his own vulnerability. They were almost at Elephant and Castle when he said, 'I can't do this any more.'

Keller looked at him, aghast.

'The job?'

'The traffic.'

He gave her a reassuring smile, then pulled the Range Rover onto the kerb and cut the corner into a side street. It took them five minutes to find an old-fashioned London boozer and they wasted no time in getting out of the rain. The place was called the Boar's Head, and it had an air of perpetual night-time about it. Oppressive black beams held up low-slung ceilings that were stained yellow from the smoke of a hundred thousand cigarettes, and the timber bar looked as if it had sailed rough seas for too long. The place was full of dark corners fit for pirates and smugglers and people who didn't want to be found. People like Foster, Abbot and Keller.

Keller sat back in the dark booth, nestled between the two men. She felt exposed, still wearing her tennis whites. Still salty from the exertion. Still knowing that her stalker was out there somewhere, lurking.

'I was thinking,' she said, 'there's no way Basilia hired that guy to scare me, or to kill Maria. I saw his eyes in the crowd. Just for a second. He was staring at me like he hated every bone in my body. I couldn't breathe when I saw that hatred burning. He's the guy. It's all about him and me. Nobody hired him. Not Basilia or anyone else. I just wish I knew why.'

Abbot swilled his beer in his glass and took a sideways glance at Foster to see if he could get a steer on his thoughts. But Foster sat impassive and inscrutable.

'He's not a player, either,' Abbot said. 'You smashed through him yesterday like he was made of paper. He's no kind of athlete at all.'

'Okay,' Foster said, nursing his pint. 'So we know who he's not. But who the hell *is* he? And what does he want?'

'Some of those Chinese betting syndicates can get pretty nasty,' Abbot said. 'Any of them offered you money to throw a game?'

Keller shook her head.

'They wouldn't approach Kirsten,' Foster said.

Abbot raised an eyebrow.

'You sure?'

Foster turned to Keller.

'How much sponsorship did you earn last year?'

Keller looked at him for a moment.

'I didn't earn any,' Foster said, 'if it makes you feel better about disclosing.'

She smiled and said, 'Eighteen million dollars, give or take.'

Abbot gave a low whistle.

'Next round's on you,' he said.

'There's five point eight million prize money on top of that,' Foster said. 'Any gambling syndicate would know there's no point trying to bribe Kirsten. It would cost too much.'

He rolled his pint glass between his fingers, feeling it scuff across a century of beer-soaked varnish on the table beneath.

'Or they could murder my coach,' Keller said, voicing Foster's unspoken thought. 'And send me half crazy in the meantime.'

Foster nodded.

'It's possible. But there are much easier ways of getting the job done. Whatever is happening, we need to react. Today.'

Suddenly Keller looked overwhelmed.

'What are we supposed to do, if we don't even know what this guy wants?'

Foster sighed.

'You want my professional opinion?'

She said that she did.

'Go home.'

The intimacy of the past few days made the brevity of his answer sting. For a moment Keller sat in stunned silence.

'Because?'

'Because, like you say, we don't know what this is,' he said. 'Tom's right. The guy's not a player, but somehow he's got unusual access to you. He threatened you, but killed Maria. We don't know why, but the trouble hasn't stopped since she died, which means the guy is still fixated on you. He's dangerous, and he's coming. The safest thing to do is to get out of the way.'

Abbot turned to Keller and backed up his friend.

'Chris is right,' he said. 'This guy's getting closer and it looks as though he's focusing on the final.'

Keller twisted in her seat and faced Foster full on, her eyes burning into his.

'I can't control what happens when you're out on the court,' Foster told her, his voice a low admission. 'I can't promise to keep you safe. So you need to go home.'

Keller took a breath and composed herself. As Foster watched, she found her nerve. Her skin flushed, suddenly glowing healthily under the dim yellow lights. Her shoulders broadened as her lungs filled and her whole frame set in a stronger, more perfect poise. Slowly, the cold-steel gaze that Foster had seen in her eyes during matches replaced the burning anger.

'I am twenty-three years old,' she said. 'This is my time. And it doesn't come around twice. It's my time to win matches, to win tournaments and to become world champion. You know who says so? Maria Rosario. Except that she's dead. But I'll tell you something: if I run now, I will never find out who killed her, and I'll never know why. And we'll never catch this guy, and I'll live the rest of my life looking over my shoulder.'

Foster nodded.

'You know what, Chris?' Keller continued. 'Maria told me once that she quit coaching Marta Basilia because she couldn't stay objective after they slept together. And I can see that in your eyes, right now. So you need to forget everything that's happened between us and do your job. You're going to keep me safe, and we're going to nail this guy. We're going to do both of those things for Maria. Now drink up, I'll wait in the car.'

She swiped Foster's keys off the table and headed for the door. Foster swallowed his beer, avoiding eye contact with Tom Abbot. He stood up and followed Keller, lengthening his stride to keep her in sight. The words *everything that's happened between us* were still hanging in the air and, at Foster's side, Tom Abbot was supressing a smile.

'Whatever you're about to say,' Foster told him as they walked, 'don't.'

CHAPTER 22

FOSTER ENJOYED THE DRIVE back to the hotel. Abbot was riding shot-gun and Keller had strapped herself into the back. The skies had cleared and the summer rain was starting to steam off the tarmac. Keller's new-found strength was invigorating and his mood had lifted.

'One of us can stay with you at all times over the next couple of days,' he told her. 'Once you're on the court you'll be exposed, obviously, but I can reach you in seven seconds if I'm sitting in the front few rows.'

'Don't you take me off the court,' Keller warned him as they thundered under the railway bridges at Vauxhall. 'Not in the final. I'm going to win this for Maria.'

Foster locked eyes on Keller in the rear-view mirror.

'If you're in danger, I couldn't give a damn about Maria Rosario's legacy, or your prize money, or anything else. I'll drag you off that court, if it's the right thing to do.'

At Foster's request, Abbot kept his eyes on Keller all afternoon. She spent most of the time in her suite, calling her family and arranging her travel plans for after the final. Then she dedicated some time to a few more episodes of *Better Call Saul*. She educated Abbot as they went along, explaining *Breaking Bad* back-stories about Walter White and people cooking meth in their underpants.

Foster needed some space to think, so he drove over to the quiet solitude of Highgate Cemetery. The skies stayed blue and the warm sunlight threw sharp, contrasting shadows over the white-marble carvings. Angels looked down on him and the breeze carried the sounds of songbirds and tousled the creeping ivy, as unchecked nature slowly claimed the stone back for itself. If there was a definition of peace, this was it.

The gravestone stood testament to his royal client's gratitude for saving his life three years ago. But it didn't change the fact that Elaina was gone. He rested his back against the cold stone and closed his eyes, talking to her about the list of things that had happened since he last visited. He didn't bring flowers, because he couldn't bear the thought of them slowly decaying, the way every beautiful thing in nature eventually did. Besides, he had given Elaina flowers so rarely when she was alive that any overblown gesture now would make her spirit suspicious. *With good reason*, he thought, as his mind turned to Kirsten Keller.

In the calm oasis he slowly unravelled Keller's story. He described his frustration at not being able to keep her safe, and his sense of foreboding. Elaina listened as she always did, never in any rush as she lay quietly between the humming dragonflies and the gentle rustling leaves. And she told him what he already knew: that he was good at his job, but he cared too much. And she told him that no matter how much he risked to keep Keller safe, none of it would convince her to rise from the dead and come back to him.

'You're on your own, kiddo,' she said, and Foster smiled.

He returned to the Shard in the early evening and took Keller to dinner in Oblix, a New York grill on the thirty-second floor. Choosing from the menu proved a challenge. Keller ordered carefully, according to her diet, but she still pushed most of what the kitchen had prepared around her plate, just as she had at The Ivy.

Foster ate well, feeling unburdened after his conversation with Elaina. Time moved on, just as Keller had told him, in the bedroom in the Shangri-La. He couldn't bring Elaina back, and he couldn't be all things to all people. But finally he felt ready to move forward. He savoured the feeling of good food in his belly and, once Kirsten was safely in bed, took up his position on the sofa in the outer room and fell into a deep and dreamless sleep.

CHAPTER 23

THE WOODBRIDGE HOTEL WAS a four-storey red-brick building less than a mile from the All England Lawn Tennis Club. Each of the rounded burgundy blinds hovering above the metal-framed windows was covered in pigeon-shit and greyed by the fumes of the traffic below. Behind the palm-smeared glass of the aluminium doors, a shabby reception area greeted guests with the smell of wet dog and cheap air freshener.

The Woodbridge was not the kind of place that employed especially attentive lobby staff, which was good, as far as the man crossing the worn blue carpet was concerned. He walked briskly with a faint limp. A livid purple bruise was still maturing on the side of his neck. He had considered turning up his collar to conceal the injury, but he decided against it, figuring he would only draw more attention to himself. Anyway, the receptionist had little interest in passing guests. He had barely looked up from his *Racing Post* when the bruised man left the hotel, and he had not looked up at all when the man returned, crossed the lobby and disappeared into the rickety lift that ascended swiftly to the floor where he was staying.

The man had only left the hotel for a matter of minutes. He walked the short journey along the main road and into a side street, where he found Green's Hardware Store. The place was a cornucopia of screws and nails and duct tape, and replacement parts for lawnmowers and vacuum cleaners. The man found what he was looking for towards the back of the shop: a studded hardboard display of polished metal blades. There were bushcraft and wood-carving knives, machetes and axes. The way they were displayed together, hidden in a dark corner of this unassuming shop, it was hard to believe that anyone bought them for their original and stated purpose.

He chose a matt-black hunting knife that glinted silver along its razor-sharp edge and curved to a vicious point. It looked sturdy enough to do the job, and stealthy enough that he could fold it away and carry it without being noticed. Perfect. An old guy with an impressive grey moustache had been only too happy to remove and box the display model, asking no questions and avoiding all eye contact. His gaze lingered for a moment on the man's bruised neck, before he dropped the goods into a brown paper bag, which the man tucked under his arm before paying cash and leaving the shop.

Back in his room in the Woodbridge, he unwrapped the box and took the knife in his hand, feeling the weight of it. He liked it almost as much as his old one, which he had lost when the bodyguard had smashed it from his hand inside the tennis club. That had been a close call. And yet he had survived it and here he was, so close to completing the job. He looked at himself in the dull mirror that had been screwed to the wall for at least twenty years. He held the black knife up in front of his face, so that his cold eyes were scowling back at him from either side of the blade.

Until yesterday the mirror had been decorated by the silver chain that he had stolen from Maria Rosario's neck after he killed her, and he had smiled every time he looked at it, because he had imagined the look of terror he would see in Keller's face when he put the chain in her hands. Reality had not disappointed.

He had expected to feel guilty about Rosario. In all honesty, she was not to blame for what had happened, but in the end he had not found it hard to kill her. It was all part of the plan. And tomorrow he would do the job for which he had been preparing for the past twelve months.

He looked at the blade again and ran the tip of his finger across the gleaming edge. He thought about his brother. Remembered how they played together as kids. Remembered his father telling him that nothing in life mattered more than looking out for his kid brother. Remembered watching as the sheriff's department cut Jake down from the motel ceiling, when they found him blue and lifeless. Remembered Kirsten Keller smiling on the TV in the motel room as she won Wimbledon. The last thing Jake ever saw. She hadn't even bothered to come home for the funeral.

The man smiled as he realised the blade had scoured his skin, and a thin ribbon of blood was trickling down his finger and across his palm. People say revenge only hollows you out. That's bullshit. Killing Rosario had given him a buzz, and killing Keller would be a million times better. He might not live beyond tomorrow, but that was okay. Either way, by tomorrow he would be free.

CHAPTER 24

DESPITE ALL THE PLANNING, when Kirsten Keller walked out onto Centre Court for the final, Foster felt on edge. The court was wide open, and she was too far from his reach. He sat two rows back from the turf, close to the chairs where Keller herself would rest between games. He knew he was getting too emotionally attached, and he knew it was a weakness. But this was the end of it. Tomorrow she'd be gone.

He watched the crowd, searching for anything suspicious. There was nothing. He watched excited fans take their seats and adjust their sunglasses and hats, preparing for a couple of hours in the afternoon heat; people smiling as they squeezed uncomfortably close to each other as they passed in the aisles. Foster turned in his seat and made one last sweep across the crowd behind him. As he did so, his eyes settled on a guy in his late twenties coming up late through the nearest olive-green entrance. He looked cagey, his dark eyes taking in the scene carefully. Every other person who had surfaced from the sunken entrance had instantly smiled. It was a natural reaction, Foster figured, when suddenly emerging into one of the world's most famous sporting arenas. But this guy didn't smile. He turned towards Foster as if he could sense his stare. For a moment their eyes connected, and time froze. Then, for no apparent reason, the guy turned on his heel and headed swiftly back down the tunnel.

Foster rose on instinct and followed.

'The match is about to begin, sir,' a woman in a smart black jacket and a peaked cap told him as he pushed through the exit door. Foster kept walking, entering a walkway flecked by the last few excited stragglers heading towards their seats, and one man walking briskly away from them. He had a similar build to the guy who had followed him through the grounds after the quarter finals. He slipped out of the walkway and into the bright concourse, and skirted around the outside of Centre Court as Foster followed.

'Hey!' Foster called out.

The guy didn't turn round. Instead, he broke his stride and began to run, gently at first, but as he sensed Foster following, he increased his speed. The milling crowd began to thicken, until eventually the concourse spread out onto the wide-open grass that the fans had christened 'Henman Hill' back in the Noughties and had rechristened 'Murray Mound' a decade later. A huge screen loomed over the lawn, and fans were watching the opening game of the final. The crowd was broiling and churning in the sunshine, a mass of elegant strawberry-munchers and Pimm's-swillers and picnickers and raucous hen-dos, wearing everything from tennis whites to garish fancy-dress outfits. But each of them was focused on the action on the screen, and none of them made way when the guy Foster was chasing ploughed into them. He got stuck in the crowd, snared by the tangle of their limbs.

Foster was on him in seconds. He grabbed the man's wrist and forced his arm behind his back. The guy yelled and a few onlookers backed off, the violence an unwelcome novelty inside the serenity of the All England Lawn Tennis Club.

'Video this,' the man yelled to anyone who would listen. His anger accentuated his east-London accent. 'Grab your phones, put this on YouTube – seriously. This is police brutality, man.'

A few people turned to see what the commotion was all about, and the guy played up to them, yelling again as Foster forced his arm further up his back.

'Who are you?' Foster said, applying more pressure to the guy's wrist. 'Why did you run?'

'I ran because you're a cop,' the guy said. 'I'm not stupid. I could tell the way you looked at me that you'd rumbled me. So I legged it.'

'Rumbled you doing what?'

As Foster twisted the guy's arm harder still, his palm sprang open on reflex. A cascade of grubby entrance tickets fluttered down to the ground, spilling onto the lawn between the two men. There were murmurs in the crowd.

Shit!

'You're touting?'

'Of course I'm fucking touting,' the guy said, looking at the pile of spilled tickets. 'I'm not going to deny it now, bro, am I?'

Shit! Wrong guy. In the London sunshine, a frost crept across Foster's skin. This was the wrong time to be in the wrong place.

He let go of the guy's wrist and watched him scrabble about on the lawn, gathering up his tickets. The crowd surrounding the two men suddenly gasped and then roared, as Keller won a point on the big screen in front of them. The commentary echoed across the lawn as the pundits filled the seconds between points.

'That's a great shot from Keller,' an Australian voice said. 'Incredible precision for the first game. Brave, too.'

CHAPTER 25

FOSTER HALF TURNED TOWARDS the screen. The camera zoomed in on Keller. She looked focused and calm. Foster wished he felt the same way.

'Yes, I think we can see the umpire taking a second look at that, as it hits the line,' said a second, English voice as a slow-mo played through on the screen. 'But you can see chalk dust fly up as the ball lands, so it was a good call from the line judge.'

The crowd around Foster and the tout had gone back to watching the big screen, too, happy to disengage from the momentary unpleasantness.

'Big day for Noah Saunders,' the commentary continued. 'He's been given the umpire's chair for the final at short notice, due to Rachel Clapham being taken ill. He comes from a tennis family. His brother was a talented player, but sadly he took his own life a year ago today.'

Keller bounced the ball on the service line, and the crowd hushed. The commentator continued in quiet tones.

'Yes, it must have been a roller coaster of a year for Noah Saunders, and it's good to see him in the chair today.'

Keller fired into the net and the crowd on the lawn groaned.

'Helluva bruise on his neck, mind you,' said the Australian. 'Looks like he's been in the wars.'

Someone in the TV gallery must have been listening because the picture cut to a view of the umpire, and a livid purple bruise on the side of his neck. And in that moment Foster's instinct was triggered. He was about to turn back to Centre Court when he felt the presence of someone behind him, and turned to see a broad-shouldered security guard at his back. Another guard arrived behind the ticket tout.

'Is everything okay, gentlemen?'

The tout swore under his breath.

'Fine,' Foster said. 'I need to get back inside Centre.'

The guards didn't move.

'Can I ask what the altercation was about, sir?'

He was professional, and his courteous attitude seemed genuine enough. But Foster didn't have time for it.

'This guy's touting. I saw him, and he ran.'

The guard looked from Foster to the other man, then nodded to his two colleagues, who escorted the tout away from Murray Mound towards the exits. Over the guard's shoulder the big screen was still showing the Centre Court action. Keller looked fine. Composed. The live feed cut to a shot of the scoreboard. Thirty all, first game. Not that the score mattered to Foster any more.

'Sir, I need to take some details from you.'

Foster snapped back to his situation on Murray Mound.

'What details?' he said, already beginning to move towards Centre Court.

'Whenever there's an incident,' the guard said, walking alongside Foster, 'we have to fill in a log. You have to sign it.'

Foster broke into a jog.

'I'm sorry,' he said. 'I don't have time.'

The guard got physical, really quickly. He put a restraining hand on the arm of Foster's jacket and reached to grab his shoulder with the other.

'I'm sorry, sir,' he said, 'but it's our policy that anyone—'

He never finished the sentence. Foster twisted out of the guy's grip and kicked his legs from under him. The guard was a mass of muscle, and he fell hard. Foster put a knee between his shoulder blades and then patted him on the back as he faced the ground.

'I'm really sorry,' he said to him. 'But I've absolutely got to go. You'll understand later, trust me.'

Foster pushed up and away, and by the time the guard got to his feet and reached for the radio on his lapel, Foster was out of sight. Another guard tried to stop him at the entrance to the court, but Foster pushed past.

An excited hush descended over the crowd and Foster's feet scuffed audibly as he made his way quickly towards his seat. He looked at the umpire, perched on top of the green chair, high above the action. Foster could see the livid purple bruise on the left side of his neck. A bruise that could have been caused by being punched hard in the throat.

On the court, Kirsten Keller smashed a forehand just inside the white line for a clean winner and the stadium erupted. But Foster didn't see it. His eyes were locked, unblinking, on the umpire. Was he the same guy he'd bowled into outside Court 12? He was the right age. The right build. And an umpire would have access to the locker rooms. An umpire would follow the tour around the world.

Game point. Keller cannoned a serve dead-centre. Her opponent smashed it back at her, but the ball drifted wide of the line and the crowd cheered.

'Game, Miss Keller,' Noah Saunders said, his voice echoing around the stadium.

The commentator had said that Saunders' brother had killed himself one year ago today. Foster pulled out his phone and searched online for more details and found an article straight away: *Heartbreak Tennis Ace Found Dead.*

The website reported that Jake Saunders, brother of respected umpire Noah Saunders and Kirsten Keller's ex-boyfriend, had been found dead in a Santa Barbara motel. A good player, the report said, but not great enough to join Keller on the world tour, and the couple had gone their separate ways. Jake had not coped well, and not long after the break-up he had hanged himself, with Keller's tennis matches playing on the TV screen in front of him.

The same way Maria Rosario had died.

The umpire looked edgy, shifting in his smart blue blazer and fidgeting with his hands. Foster knew that Saunders had crafted this moment. No doubt he had poisoned the match umpire to get in the chair. He had terrorised Keller and killed Maria Rosario. All of it had been building up to today, the anniversary of his younger brother's suicide. Foster slipped his phone back into his pocket and braced himself for what was coming.

CHAPTER 26

FOSTER HAD NO JURISDICTION to climb over the barriers and onto the court. By the time he was halfway there, he'd be wrestled to the ground by fifteen well-meaning security guys, and while he was on the ground Noah Saunders would have time to act.

Oblivious to it all, Kirsten Keller was completely still at the far end of the court. Her razor-stare was fixed on her opponent. It was break point and she sensed blood. Her opponent served. They were seventy-eight feet apart. Keller had a little less than half a second to react. Duly the ball came, and she flung herself at it and returned it deep into her opponent's half of the court. It was unreturnable, and the crowd erupted.

'Game, Miss Keller.'

Noah Saunders leaned forward and began to rise from his chair. Some of the applause turned to concerned shouts, as sections of the crowd spotted the glint of a blade emerging from his jacket. Now it was Foster's turn to react at lightning speed. No official gets out of the chair during a match, so Foster was already moving before he saw the knife. With no concrete plan, he ran straight at the umpire's chair and flung himself at it. He leapt high, shouldering it well above its centre of gravity. The whole thing toppled sideways under his weight.

Foster landed hard, partly on the wooden frame of the chair. Ignoring the pain, he forced himself up off the ground and towards Saunders, who had fallen a few yards in front of him. Foster grabbed at his legs, but Saunders turned and slashed the sharp blade at him. Foster's arm sprang back involuntarily when he felt a white-hot slash across his flesh. Saunders threw himself at Keller, grabbing her by the hair and pulling her roughly to him. He put the knife to her throat.

The crowd screamed now, falling over each other to pour through the exits. Foster could see them draining out like sand in an hourglass. As he watched, Saunders slipped a noose of twine from his blazer pocket. He pulled it over Kirsten's head and twisted it in his fist, holding her close like a human shield, biting into her hair so that she couldn't pull her head away.

When she felt his teeth in her hair, Keller reacted, leaning forward slightly and then smashing her head backwards with everything she'd got. Even above the noise of the horrified crowd, there was a crunch. Noah Saunders spat angrily and dug the knife under her jawbone. When he looked out from behind her, his lip was split and there was a yawning gap where a couple of his teeth should have been. Blood began to pour down his chin and onto his shirt.

Foster weighed up his options. In the stands, creeping forward in Saunders' blind spot, a uniformed policeman had drawn a bright-yellow Taser and was holding it steadily with both hands as he vaulted in slow motion over the chairs in front of him.

Foster said, 'Kirsten, look at me. This is all going to be alright.'

Noah Saunders laughed.

'I can promise you it's not going to be alright, Kirsten. Especially for you.'

Foster was suddenly aware that his palm was wet and he looked down to see it slashed from the base of his thumb right across his palm, deep enough to expose sinew and bone. In the corner of his eye he could see the policeman getting closer. All the guy needed was a clear shot. Foster tried to engineer one.

'Do you think this is what your brother would want?' Foster asked, hoping the mention of his brother would cause Saunders to react.

Keller looked stricken, as she suddenly realised what all this was about.

'What do you want from me?' she said to Saunders, her head tilted backwards from the pressure of the knife under her jaw. 'I only knew Jake for a few months. I'm sorry you lost him, but it wasn't my fault.'

'He loved you.'

'I never asked him to.'

Foster watched Keller and Saunders, thinking fast. Saunders had killed Rosario, and now he was out in the open, with Keller in his grasp. He wasn't going to stop. Not unless someone stopped him.

'You're an embarrassment to your brother.' Foster went in hard. 'If he loved Kirsten, this is the last thing he'd want.'

The goading worked. Saunders stepped out from behind Keller so that he could point at Foster with his blade.

The cop with the Taser took his chance, shouting, 'Armed Police', and fired as the umpire spun towards him. But he missed, instead hooking Keller with the high-voltage wire. She stiffened and shook, every muscle in her body pulling taut and convulsing. She toppled backwards, only Saunders' firm grip on the noose keeping her on her feet. Her eyes bulged and her head twisted awkwardly under the strain.

Saunders pulled her back close to him, shielding himself once more.

'You fucking missed,' he spat at the cop. 'Now back off or I'll slit her throat.'

The cop did as he was told.

Saunders reached round and ripped the metal wire from Keller's skin. She screamed, and after a couple of seconds blood began to soak through her white playing top.

'That goes for the rest of you as well,' Saunders shouted across the stadium, as he spotted the red dot of a laser skirting across his forearm, and followed the beam up to a police marksman on the roof.

Then he turned to Foster.

'My brother died because of this bitch,' Saunders said. 'And today I'm putting that right. The service box you're standing in is your world, you understand? Move out of that box and bad things will happen.'

Foster kept his hands by his sides, and felt the blood running fast down his fingers. There was no pain from the cut in his hand or the ripped muscles in his arm. Adrenalin worked better than codeine.

He forced himself to breathe slowly as he watched Saunders walk backwards off the court, his sharp knife pressed hard into Kirsten's throat. The time for anger would be later. Right now he was calm and professional, and he waited with cold-blooded patience for the first sign of an opportunity.

CHAPTER 27

FROM WHERE CHRIS FOSTER was standing, he could see the whole stadium growing up around him. He could see the last of the seats emptying, as spectators scrambled to safety. He could see Wimbledon staff slowly melting from their exit posts and being replaced by tactical firearms police.

Noah Saunders was tucked in close to Keller, and nobody could take a shot. The TV cameras swivelled as he dragged her across the grass towards the huge scoreboard, which showed Keller's name in bright-yellow letters. When Saunders stepped off the grass onto the concrete steps of the Centre Court stands, the cameraman nearest him freaked out, stepping back from his equipment and raising his hands in the air. Saunders quickly turned towards him.

'Keep filming!' he said.

The cameraman stepped out from behind the camera, his arms raised in surrender.

'Keep fucking filming!' Saunders growled.

'It's my job to film sport,' the cameraman said. 'I don't want any part of whatever this is.'

His voice was thin and nervous, but he stood his ground. Saunders snapped. He leaned forward and grabbed the camera and smashed it hard into the cameraman's face. The cameraman dropped to his knees, holding his face in his hands. The whole thing took two seconds.

But two seconds was all Chris Foster needed.

He saw his chance and exploded across the court towards Saunders. By the time the umpire realised what was happening, Foster had covered half of the ground between them and was still accelerating. Keller could see him coming, and as Saunders grabbed for her again, she used all the strength she had left to smash into her tormentor for the second time that afternoon, knocking the wind out of him and causing him to topple backwards.

Police marksmen, who had been slowly edging along the gantries high above, began calling sharp instructions to each other as the situation below them suddenly changed. Saunders ignored them, his mind fixed on finishing the job. He scrambled from underneath Keller and punched her hard in the ribs, pulling her up by her hair and dragging her up the flight of concrete stairs. It was hopeless; Foster was almost on him. As Saunders reached the top of the stairs he could almost feel Foster's breath, so he took the only option he had left. He pushed the tip of the knife into Kirsten Keller's throat. It cut deep enough to draw blood, a gentle river pooling on the blade and then dripping slowly down onto her whites.

Foster froze, as he knew he had to, and Saunders pulled Keller through into the players' box. But Foster was aware of the net tightening around all of them, with the police teams repositioning and drawing slowly closer.

'You know the problem with all of this?' he told Saunders. 'My guess is that your brother loved her. Loved the bones of her. Loved her enough to kill himself. This is not what he would want.'

Saunders looked for a moment as if he had seen reason, and he slowly straightened up, lowered the knife and eased Keller away from him. Foster sprinted into the players' box to grab her, but at the last second Saunders shoved her hard in the back and she toppled sideways over the edge of the balcony with the noose around her neck.

Foster dived to grab her and stop her neck from snapping as the rope went taut. He managed to clasp her bicep with his left hand, but her weight wrenched his injured arm. The strain pulled at the scar tissue, bending and twisting the titanium plates screwed to the remains of his bones. Keller's legs scrabbled in vain as she dangled in front of the scoreboard. Foster reached over with his right arm to pull her to safety, but Saunders lunged at him with the knife. Foster only just managed to turn back in time to deflect the blade and push Saunders away.

He knew he couldn't hold onto Keller and hold off Saunders. White light sparked across his vision and the air fled from his lungs in a gasp of agony. Saunders was keeping low enough behind the barrier to avoid the marksmen's laser dots, which were dancing around the players' box, and resolutely held onto the rope in his hand. Foster's arm was failing, and he could feel Kirsten slipping further into the noose.

He looked into Saunders' vicious eyes. The same eyes Keller had seen flash with hatred from within the crowd of fans after the semi-final. The same eyes that had watched Maria Rosario die. As Saunders launched at him again, Foster used his free arm to swing the heaviest punch he could muster at the guy's eye socket. The punch connected and threw Saunders backwards, just far enough that the marksmen were able to finally fix their red dots on his body. Three of them hit. Two bore deep holes in his chest. The third caved in his head and instantly matted his hair with grey and red.

Foster was still holding onto Keller's arm, his shoulder slowly being pulled out of its socket. There was a good chance it was already out, but he was beyond differentiating one pain from another. Then he heard Abbot's voice down below.

'Let her go, Chris. I've got her.'

He opened his fist and felt Keller's arm slide through his hand as she fell. He guessed the drop was a couple of yards, and he trusted Abbot to catch her. He heard her scream and then heard Abbot reassuring her, and was aware of his own harsh breathing for the first time since he'd chased after Noah Saunders. He rolled back over the barrier, falling in a heap onto the concrete floor.

He lay on his back for a long moment and looked up at the steel rafters and let out an exhausted primal scream. It was a cacophony of agony, relief and delirious pleasure that it was over, and that they were all still alive.

CHAPTER 28

THE POLICE INTERVIEWED THEM all night, Foster helping them to piece together what had happened with the murder of Maria Rosario.

They slept through most of the morning, Keller stretched out in the king-sized bed, and Foster and Abbot taking a sofa each in the outer room. When her need to eat began to outweigh her need to sleep, Keller emerged in the doorway in her underwear and a tight white T-shirt. She strolled over to them and melted into Foster's arms, despite his protestations and Tom Abbot's wide grin.

'I'm going to make myself scarce,' Abbot said, pulling his jacket from the back of a chair and straightening the lapels over his chest.

'You're going nowhere,' Keller told him, and she turned back to Foster and looked up into his calm eyes. Hers were clear and bright, the weight of the past few weeks suddenly lifted. 'We're alive,' she said. 'And that's something to celebrate. I'm twenty-three years old and I haven't had a drink for as long as I can remember. And I'm hungry for the first time in a month.'

'Call it intuition,' Foster said, 'but would you like us to take you to lunch?'

She smiled more widely than Foster had ever seen and headed off to get changed. He booked a table on the thirty-second floor and they drank cocktails before lunch. Even with Abbot in tow, Foster found it hard to resist the urge to take hold of Kirsten Keller's hand as they stood next to each other in the lift.

The rolling news on the TV screens above the bar showed clips of Foster charging across Centre Court and bowling into the umpire's chair. They ignored it and dug deeper into the drinks menu.

Abbot had a plane to catch mid-afternoon. He clasped hands with Foster, firmer friends than ever, and promised he wouldn't leave it three years next time.

When Foster came back to Kirsten, she was watching the London sky, which had clouded over and was suddenly grey and forbidding.

'I hardly knew Jake Saunders,' she said, 'let alone Noah. We only went out for a few months. When I heard he'd killed himself, I couldn't believe it.'

Foster watched as her brow furrowed.

'You must have been upset?'

'Sure. But I was confused, too. I mean, we weren't soulmates. We weren't life partners. It was no big deal, as far as I knew. Does that make me a complete bitch?'

Foster shook his head.

'Not at all. I guess Jake Saunders was just a time-bomb waiting to go off.'

Keller's eyes warmed with gratitude.

'Same as his brother. I keep thinking that if I hadn't gone out with Jake, Maria would still be alive.'

Foster shook his head.

'Thinking like that will drive you mad,' he said. 'I know. I did it for three years. Who knows how many times you saved Maria's life? Maybe she coached you one day, rather than catching a bus that plunged over a cliff. Or maybe if you hadn't offered to work with her, Basilia might have accidentally tripped her down the stairs one day. You can't trace consequence to a single action. The bottom line is that a guy decided to kill Maria, and that's his responsibility, not yours.'

She turned down the corners of her mouth and cocked her head to one side, as if she was trying to believe him, but couldn't quite let herself off the hook.

'Thank you for what you did. I'll never forget it.'

Foster shrugged.

'It's my job.'

'Just your job?'

He held her gaze, but said nothing. Eventually she smiled and the worry began to lift from her face.

'Just doing your job,' she said. 'That's such a cliché.'

Foster smiled.

'There's no pleasing some people.'

They ordered food, and for once Kirsten Keller demolished hers without looking up from her plate.

'You sure I couldn't tempt you to join my team?' she said after dessert. 'I could show you the world.'

Foster shook his head.

'I've seen enough of it already, Kirsten.'

She smiled, unsurprised by his answer.

Their eyes locked for a moment, both of them imagining how it could be, if they were together.

'Well,' Keller said eventually, 'if you ever change your mind . . .'

They both smiled, and Foster went back to watching the sky.

'When do you fly?' Foster asked.

'Tomorrow.'

'Straight home?'

She shook her head.

'I'm taking a few days in Florence. Maria's family are flying her home, and her funeral is next week. I want to be there. Basilia's coming, too. I guess some things are more important than tennis.'

'Will you replay the final?' Foster asked.

She shook her head.

'I'll come back if they can organise it,' she said. 'But I don't think they will.'

Foster told her she'd win the next tournament, and she told him he could bank on it, suddenly sassy and confident.

'Do you feel safe now?' Foster asked her.

'I'd feel safer if you stayed tonight,' she said, and her eyes sparkled like the late sunshine glinting on the Thames far below.

Detective Harriet Blue picks up a case that comes shockingly close to home

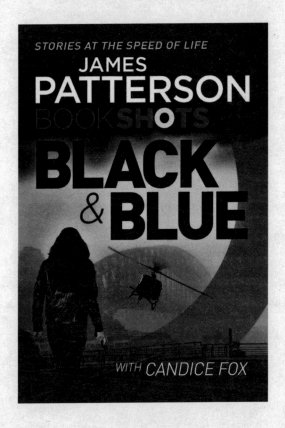

Available now!

I'M AN EXPERIENCED HUNTER of humans. It's not hard, if you understand how they think. People have tunnel vision and are objective-driven. As long as you don't interfere with their goal, and don't make yourself known before you're ready to pounce, you can close in on a relaxed target pretty easily. It doesn't even require much stealth. Unlike animals, human beings don't use their alarm system of senses. Though the wind was behind me, Ben Hammond didn't smell me. He didn't hear my breath over the clunk of his boots on the pavement.

Hammond's objective was his late-model Honda Civic on the edge of the parking lot. So that's all he could see – he didn't notice me round the corner from the loading dock and fall into step behind him. He left the shopping centre with hands full of groceries swinging at his sides and headed across the parking lot, already sliding into the driver's seat in his mind, shutting the door on the moonless night.

I followed with my head down, the hoodie pulled up against the security cameras trained on the few remaining cars. I let him pull his keys out of his pocket, the jangling sound covering the soft fall of my boots for the last few steps between me and my prey.

I closed the distance and attacked.

'FUCK!' BEN HAMMOND GRABBED at the back of his head where I'd punched him, turned and stumbled against the car, dropping the bags. Glass cracked in one of them. He cowered in a half-crouch, trying to make himself smaller. Both hands shot up. 'Oh my God! What are you doing?'

'Stand up,' I waved impatiently.

'Take my wallet,' he stammered. 'Don't hurt m—'

'You don't like the surprise attack, do you, Ben? You know how effective it is.'

He realised three things very quickly. First, that I was a woman. Second, that this wasn't a mugging. Third, that he'd heard my voice before.

The man straightened almost fully and squinted into the darkness of my hood. I tugged the hood down and watched his eyes wander around the silhouette of my short hair against the shopping-centre lights, the terror in his face slowly dissipating.

'I . . .' He straightened. His hands dropped. 'I know you.'

'You do.'

'You're that cop.' He pointed an uncertain finger at me, began to shake it as his confidence grew. 'You're that cop from the trial.'

'I am,' I said. 'Detective Harriet Blue, here to deliver your punishment.'

IT WAS A LITTLE insulting that my name didn't come to Ben's mind as quickly as I'd hoped. But I had just cracked him on the skull. What little grey matter was sloshing around his brain probably needed time to recover. I'd done everything I could to make him aware of me while he was tried for the rape of his ex-girlfriend Molly. When I took to the stand to testify that I'd found Molly at the bottom of the shower where he'd dumped her, I'd looked right at him and calmly and clearly stated my name.

It hadn't been a solid case. Ben had been very crafty in getting back at his ex for leaving him: raping and beating her, but charming his way into her apartment struggle-free and sharing a glass of wine with her first, so it looked as if she'd welcomed the sexual encounter. I'd known, sitting on the witness stand and staring at him, that like most rapists he'd probably go free.

But that didn't mean I was finished with him.

'This is assault.' Ben touched the back of his head, noted the blood on his fingers and almost smiled. 'You're in a lot of trouble, you stupid little bitch.'

'Actually,' I slid my right foot back, '*you're* in a lot of trouble.'

I gave Ben a couple of sharp jabs to the face, then backed up, let him have a moment to feel them. He stepped out from between the shopping bags and came at me swinging. I sidestepped and planted my knee in his ribs, sending him sprawling on the asphalt. I glanced at the distant shopping centre. The security guards would notice a commotion at the edge of the furthest parking lot camera and come running. I figured I had seconds, not minutes.

'You can't do this.' Hammond spat blood from his split lip. 'You—'

I gave him a knee to the ribs, then lifted him before he could get a lungful of air and slammed him into the bonnet. I'm petite, but I box, so I know how to manoeuvre a big opponent. I grabbed a handful of Ben's hair and dragged him towards the driver's door.

'You're a cop!' Hammond wailed.

'You're right,' I said. I could just make out two security guards rushing out of the loading dock.

'My job gives me access to crime alerts,' I said. 'I can tag a person's file and get a notification every time they're brought in, even if their original charge never stuck.'

I held on to Hammond's hair and gave him a couple of hard punches in the head, then dumped him onto the ground. The guards were closer. I stepped on Hammond's balls, so I knew I had his full attention.

'If I ever see your name in the system again,' I told him, 'I'm coming back. And I won't be this gentle next time.'

I pulled my hood up and sprinted into the scrubland at the side of the lot.

I'M NOT A VIGILANTE. Sometimes I just have no choice but to take matters into my own hands.

I'd worked in sex crimes for five years, and I was tired of seeing predators walking free from convictions. When I got close to a victim, the way I did with Molly Finch, I found it hard to sleep after their attacker was acquitted. For weeks I'd lain awake at night thinking about Hammond's smug face as he'd walked down the steps of the courthouse on Goulburn Street, the wink he'd given me as he got into the taxi. I'd managed to make a minor physical assault charge stick. But there had been no proving *beyond a reasonable doubt* that the sex Hammond had had with Molly that night hadn't been consensual.

That's how it goes sometimes with sexual assaults. The guy's lawyer throws everything he has at the idea that she might have wanted it. There was no physical evidence, or witnesses, to say otherwise.

Well, now there was no evidence to say Ben Hammond wasn't bashed half to death by a mugger gone nuts, either. If he went to the cops about what I'd done, he'd know what it felt like not to be believed.

But he wouldn't go to the cops and tell them a woman had given him a beatdown. His kind never did.

I rolled my shoulders as I drove back across the city towards Potts Point, sighing long and low as the tension eased. I was really looking forward to getting some sleep. Most nights saw me at my local gym pounding boxing bags to try to exhaust myself into a healthy pre-sleep calm. Smacking Ben around had given me the same delicious fatigue in my muscles. I hoped it lasted.

At the big intersection near Kings Cross, a pair of hookers strutted across the road in front of my car. Their skin was lit pink by the huge neon Coca-Cola sign on the corner. The streets were still damp from a great storm the night before. The gutters were crowded with trash and huge fig-tree leaves.

My phone rang. I recognised the number as my station chief.

'Hello, Pops,' I said.

'Blue, take down this address,' the old man said. 'There's a body I want you to look at.'

MURDER WAS HARD WORK, but Hope had never been afraid of that.

She knelt on the floor of the kitchen of the *Dream Catcher* and scrubbed at the polished boards. She was trying to push her brush down the cracks and bring up the blood that had dried and settled there. *Deck*, she thought suddenly, dunking the brush in the bucket of hot water and bleach beside her. On yachts, the floor was not a floor at all but a deck. The kitchen was called a *galley*. She smiled. She'd need to get used to all the terminology. There was so much to learn, being a new boat owner. She sat back on her heels and wiped the sweat from her brow. She'd give the blood a rest for a while and work on the bedroom.

The young woman climbed backwards down the little ladder and walked into the yacht's expansive bedroom, gathering up a garbage bag from the roll she'd placed on the bed. The first thing she did was take a framed photograph from the nightstand and dump it in the darkness of the bag. She didn't look at the couple's smiling faces. She threw in some reading glasses, a pair of slippers and a folded newspaper. She opened the cupboard and started taking out the woman's clothes, grabbing great handfuls on coat hangers and bundling the shirts, skirts and pants into a roll before she shoved them into the bag.

Jenny Spelling had awful taste, Hope thought, glancing at a turquoise skirt-suit before it went into the trash. Ugh, shoulder pads. So eighties. She felt a wave of excitement roll over her as she looked along the empty hanging pole, thinking about her own clothes racked there.

When she'd filled all the garbage bags on the rolls with their possessions, Hope walked to the back of the boat to check on her prisoners. The couple were slumped in the corner of the shower cubicle, Jenny's head twisted back against the wall so that her nose pointed upward and her mouth hung open. When Hope opened the door, Ken shifted up as much as his binds would allow. His wife was limp against him.

'I'm just heading out to get rid of some rubbish,' Hope said brightly. 'You guys need anything before I go? More water?'

Jenny Spelling woke and immediately started shivering. She stared at Hope wordlessly, as though she didn't know what the young woman was.

'Hope.' Ken's face reddened with desperation. 'I'm begging you, please, just take the boat. Take everything. My wife needs to do her dialysis or she's going to die. OK? It's only going to take a few minutes. That's all. That—'

'We've discussed this.' Hope held up her hand, gave him a weary sigh. 'It'll all be over soon. I'm not getting into this again. The last time I let you loose, you did this.' She held up her forearm, showed him the bruise. '*Trust*, Ken. You had it, and you lost it.'

'Please, please.' Ken shifted. 'You don't need to do this. Look at her. Look at her face. She's missed her dialysis for three days now. She's not right. She's—'

Hope took the duct tape from the counter beside the toilet and ripped off a length. She placed a strip over Jenny's mouth, but gave Ken a few turns around his head. He was the feisty one. She worked emotionlessly as the tape sealed off his words.

'She's gonna die!' the man howled through the tape. 'Please!'

HEADING TO THE CRIME scene, I drove through the quiet streets of Picnic Point and up through the national park. The dark hills were spotted here and there with the gold porch lights of suburban mansions. I'd spent some time out here as a pre-teen with one of the foster families who had taken on my brother Sam and me. That is, before their adoption dream had ended.

There had been so many young families who'd attempted to integrate us that it was difficult to decide which one it had been. All I remembered was the local school and the crowds of teens in green and gold uniforms, the curious glances we'd received as we entered midway through the semester.

As usual, Sam and I had only been at the school for a few weeks. As a pair of kids who'd been in the system since we were practically toddlers, we didn't make life easy for our foster parents with our bad behaviour. It was probably me who had broken the spell by running away in the middle of the night. Or maybe it was Sam setting something on fire, or running his mouth at our potential new parents. We'd both been equally bad at school – fighting off kids who wanted to give us grief, trying to show our new teachers who was really boss. Once our new mummies and daddies realised we weren't grateful for being 'saved', the fantasy usually died. In truth, Sam and I had always preferred the group homes and institutions they shipped us to between potential adopters. More places to hide. I dreamed as I drove by the lamplit houses of what it might have been like to grow up here, if I'd been a more stable kid.

The police tape started at the edge of the main road. I was stopped by a young officer in a raincoat and flashed him my badge, only then realising that my knuckles were still wrapped.

'OK, Detective Blue, head down to the end of this road where it turns to dirt and go left along the river. You'll see the lights,' the cop said.

'The river? Shit!' I felt the fine hairs on my arms stand on end. 'Who's the victim?'

The cop waved me on. Another car was coming up behind me. I stood on the gas and zipped down the slope, almost swerving on the corner where the dirt began. I couldn't wait to get to the crime scene. If the victim was a young woman, it meant the Georges River Killer had struck again.

And I was going to get him this time.

JAMES PATTERSON
BOOK**SHOTS**
OUT THIS MONTH

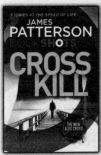

Along Came a Spider killer Gary Soneji died years ago. But Alex Cross swears he sees Soneji gun down his partner. Is his greatest enemy back from the grave?

Humans are evolving into a savage new species that could save civilisation – or end it. *Zoo* was just the beginning.

Detective Harry Blue is determined to take down the serial killer who's abducted several women, but her mission leads to a shocking revelation.

A royal is kidnapped the day before the Trooping the Colour parade. Can Private's Jack Morgan save the day before kidnap turns to murder?

A world-famous tennis player is stalked from Roland Garros to Wimbledon by a deadly killer intent on destroying more than just her career.

Two rival crews attempt to steal millions of pounds' worth of diamonds at exactly the same time, leading to a thrilling high-speed chase across Europe.

When former SAS captain David Shelley goes looking for a missing friend, he enters into the same danger that may have got his friend killed.

A man is thrown from the top floor of a glamorous new London hotel. Can Head of Security John Roscoe find the killer before the bodies pile up?

JAMES PATTERSON

BOOK**SHOTS**

COMING SOON

AIRPORT: CODE RED

A major terrorist cell sets a devastating plan in motion.
Their target? One of the world's busiest airports.

THE TRIAL: A WOMEN'S MURDER CLUB THRILLER

An accused killer will do anything to disrupt his own trial, including
a courtroom shocker that Lindsay Boxer will never see coming.

LITTLE BLACK DRESS

Can a little black dress change everything? What begins
as one woman's fantasy is about to go too far.

LEARNING TO RIDE

City girl Madeline Harper never wanted to love a cowboy. But rodeo
king Tanner Callen might change her mind... and win her heart.

ALSO BY JAMES PATTERSON

ALEX CROSS NOVELS
Along Came a Spider
Kiss the Girls
Jack and Jill
Cat and Mouse
Pop Goes the Weasel
Roses are Red
Violets are Blue
Four Blind Mice
The Big Bad Wolf
London Bridges
Mary, Mary
Cross
Double Cross
Cross Country
Alex Cross's Trial (*with Richard DiLallo*)
I, Alex Cross
Cross Fire
Kill Alex Cross
Merry Christmas, Alex Cross
Alex Cross, Run
Cross My Heart
Hope to Die
Cross Justice

THE WOMEN'S MURDER CLUB SERIES
1st to Die
2nd Chance (*with Andrew Gross*)
3rd Degree (*with Andrew Gross*)

4th of July (*with Maxine Paetro*)
The 5th Horseman (*with Maxine Paetro*)
The 6th Target (*with Maxine Paetro*)
7th Heaven (*with Maxine Paetro*)
8th Confession (*with Maxine Paetro*)
9th Judgement (*with Maxine Paetro*)
10th Anniversary (*with Maxine Paetro*)
11th Hour (*with Maxine Paetro*)
12th of Never (*with Maxine Paetro*)
Unlucky 13 (*with Maxine Paetro*)
14th Deadly Sin (*with Maxine Paetro*)
15th Affair (*with Maxine Paetro*)

DETECTIVE MICHAEL BENNETT SERIES
Step on a Crack (*with Michael Ledwidge*)
Run for Your Life (*with Michael Ledwidge*)
Worst Case (*with Michael Ledwidge*)
Tick Tock (*with Michael Ledwidge*)
I, Michael Bennett (*with Michael Ledwidge*)
Gone (*with Michael Ledwidge*)
Burn (*with Michael Ledwidge*)
Alert (*with Michael Ledwidge*)

PRIVATE NOVELS
Private (*with Maxine Paetro*)
Private London (*with Mark Pearson*)

Private Games (*with Mark Sullivan*)
Private: No. 1 Suspect (*with Maxine Paetro*)
Private Berlin (*with Mark Sullivan*)
Private Down Under (*with Michael White*)
Private L.A. (*with Mark Sullivan*)
Private India (*with Ashwin Sanghi*)
Private Vegas (*with Maxine Paetro*)
Private Sydney (*with Kathryn Fox*)
Private Paris (*with Mark Sullivan*)

NYPD RED SERIES

NYPD Red (*with Marshall Karp*)
NYPD Red 2 (*with Marshall Karp*)
NYPD Red 3 (*with Marshall Karp*)
NYPD Red 4 (*with Marshall Karp*)

STAND-ALONE THRILLERS

Sail (*with Howard Roughan*)
Swimsuit (*with Maxine Paetro*)
Don't Blink (*with Howard Roughan*)
Postcard Killers (*with Liza Marklund*)
Toys (*with Neil McMahon*)
Now You See Her (*with Michael Ledwidge*)
Kill Me If You Can (*with Marshall Karp*)

Guilty Wives (*with David Ellis*)
Zoo (*with Michael Ledwidge*)
Second Honeymoon (*with Howard Roughan*)
Mistress (*with David Ellis*)
Invisible (*with David Ellis*)
The Thomas Berryman Number
Truth or Die (*with Howard Roughan*)
Murder House (*with David Ellis*)

NON-FICTION

Torn Apart (*with Hal and Cory Friedman*)
The Murder of King Tut (*with Martin Dugard*)

ROMANCE

Sundays at Tiffany's (*with Gabrielle Charbonnet*)
The Christmas Wedding (*with Richard DiLallo*)
First Love (*with Emily Raymond*)

OTHER TITLES

Miracle at Augusta (*with Peter de Jonge*)